THE DEFINITIVE DEATH OF
PETER THE LONG

Mireya Robles

Translated by Susan Griffin
in collaboration with the author

Printed in Victoria, BC, Canada.

ISBN: 978-1-4269-1052-4 (sc)

ISBN: 978-1-4269-1053-1 (dj)

*We at Trafford believe that it is the responsibility of us all, as both individuals
and corporations, to make choices that are environmentally and socially sound.
You, in turn, are supporting this responsible conduct each time you purchase a
Trafford book, or make use of our publishing services. To find out how you are
helping, please visit www.trafford.com/responsiblepublishing.html*

*Our mission is to efficiently provide the world's finest, most comprehensive
book publishing service, enabling every author to experience success.
To find out how to publish your book, your way, and have it available
worldwide, visit us online at www.trafford.com*

Trafford rev.02/10/2010

 www.trafford.com

North America & international
toll-free: 1 888 232 4444 (USA & Canada)
phone: 250 383 6864 ♦ fax: 250 383 6804 ♦ email: info@trafford.com

The United Kingdom & Europe
phone: +44 (0)1865 487 395 ♦ local rate: 0845 230 9601
facsimile: +44 (0)1865 481 507 ♦ email: info.uk@trafford.com

10 9 8 7 6 5 4 3 2 1

ORIGINS

the pebbles at the bottom of the river, smooth, unblemished, polished, and the water washes them, runs over them with that tiny rush that she herself knows, where did these stones, eternally washing themselves in the Guaso, come from, what sands formed them, there is no air to count them, there is no sun to show them, there is no voice to detail their exact molecules for me, pressed together, pressed together till asphyxiation to form hardness, but I do know of I, of me, of these rough boots that the Guaso licks, the soles stuck to the pebbles, the water at ankle height, and my hands on my knees as van Gogh placed them when I was born in one of my many births, through the graphite of his pencil, to cry, seated in a chair, eternally leaning towards his signature, Vincent; at what moment did I leap to this rock in the Guaso to be born, seated, in my sixty fifth year, draping a peach skin about myself to cover the movement of my blood, to cover my glazed veins, dressing myself with rebellious freedom in workers' blue, the blue getting wet at the edges, at ankle height, the blue resting on a rock, the blue covering my sex which I sense dried out, the blue hugging my breast, my back, the contours of my arms, and now I am colours, and I continue disobeying, disobeying you, van Gogh, and I raise my head a little, my hands now placed on each side of the corners of my mouth, to leave the eyes free, so that you stay there, old man grieving, man of graphite, and in my peach skin, motionless, the eyes free to watch the universe pass by no-one knew where Peter "the Lame" Matei had come from, with his eternal wanderings and his space devouring eyes; they called him Peter the Lame to accommodate the customary nickname and this one was given in passing, just to call him something, because, in reality, his long, extremely long, legs were the same length; a flock of ragged children, some with enormous protuberant navels, followed Peter everywhere; they followed him to the Guaso river but the fear that they might break the Shadow of the Quietly Desperate Old Man kept them at a distance, or perhaps it was the fear that the Old Man might not be a real being, rather, something inexplicably animated and ambulatory, of whom some even said that the hairs that stuck out of his nose and ears could be an invention of all the eyes that scrutinized his figure, while others insisted that, surely, he did not even have dry mucus stuck to the inside of his nose, nor sweat in his armpits, nor rankness between his lean buttocks, because word had gone around that Peter's nose and ears and buttocks were a lie, that all of him was a lie and that he was destined, definitively, to disappear just like --as they had all witnessed-- Alka Seltzer disappeared in water; it became a ritual, going to wait for the disappearance of Peter, always keeping a distance, always from afar so as not to interrupt the sacred perimeter of his solitude; they watched him from afar, they followed him from afar, but they always followed him, because Peter, nicknamed "the Long" since he brusquely and categorically forbad that they call him "the one who was born at the right time", was, in some strange way, the direct descendent of the first landowner, as he called the earth's citizens, and there were those who also affirmed that he was the same first landowner who had descended columns of hours and minutes and appeared, like any neighbour's son, placed in the painting on a postcard that all thought they recognised but couldn't quite remember, or walking along any pathway, or appearing from the bark of a very big tree with variegated leaves that had been planted at the entrance to the town many years ago; that same morning, various children and even the odd adult declared that, in his earliest excursion, they had witnessed the air push Peter, now known as the Long, and that they saw him elevate himself to a height of ten inches above the sidewalk, slowly glide forward without touching the ground for a space of three metres, descend, walk a few steps, elevate himself to the same height, advance three more metres and descend again; Peter was unaware of the arguments and discussions that his propelling movement had provoked, some claimed they had been witnesses to what, years later, the more cultured would call Matei's *modus traslatorio,* while others insisted that it was all a farce and that various false witnesses had taken up strategic positions around the town for group support and to start lies that would blacken the town like a thick curtain of mud; Peter felt himself walking, his thinness assaulted at times by wrinkles, as any neighbour's son would walk, with strides that refused to hurry, and thinking, always thinking: "puritanical little virgins, old ladies in salmon, cod in the Gallego's corner shop, there goes that Mondonguito and I don't ask his grandmother for stale bread so that she doesn't trap my arm in the grille of the door; old arm-swallower, you keep the bread to grate it and make bread pudding, flan de pan, flanflan, pampan; Mondonguito, a crossroad, are you going to be the Club's president with that head of kinky hair you have? Mondonguito, Tribilín, don't you listen to the holy words?" that was what the teacher used to say to me, "let's see, Pete, this afternoon you're in charge of putting the chalk, paper and pencils neatly in the cupboard, after class, yes, you had to do it yerterday, yes, and the day before, yes, you've had to do it since the first day and it will continue to be your turn, but you're slow and that's why you have to do everything twice, well, yes, trice, well, yes, you are the only one who has to work, but isn't that why you're Peter the Lame?" Peter the Lame she says; I'm Matei and a poet; learned lessons in gibberish in which I carefully use the dictionary of words until they are not words but only one compact and universal word for all; and you will see: you might be the teacher, but I am Peter Matei; the children that followed the old man that morning had skin the exact colour of toasted almonds; their clothes, torn and dirty, were all the same, the colour of sand; Peter walked into the river, taking care not to slip on the polished pebbles; his arms outstretched for balance, lurches that ended in equilibrium, and at last, the enormous stone on which he would seat himself just as he had made his appearance one fine day, like any neighbour's son, out of no-where according to the dubious testimony of those who called themselves witnesses to his apparition; Peter made himself comfortable, adjusting his wide trousers, pointing, one by one, at his intrusive followers so that they would move further away until they disappeared from the area, and began, now alone, the morning's first litany: "big head, ed, ed; don't say that bad word, ord, ord; Lalitaa! Lalitaa! and who is that Lalita? it's the bicentennial bitch that is trotting through the mountains; ah! how perfect is history, ory, ory;" and now, eternal peace

THE FIRST EXPEDITION

walking, the rising sun accompanying me, the staff steadying my hand; the sandals, the full length tunic; supporting myself, resting after hours as if to calm, with my repose, the sun that was becoming intense; one must continue, one must always continue, and my feet developing the ability of desert animals to cross interminable, fine crystals, travelling through towns, the villages with their merchants; a scribe awaiting a dictation that he will quickly note down, the tax collectors, the astrologers and others who will one day be given the name of alchemists; the brief stay in each town, the basin, the water licking my pores to empty them of dust, the fresh fruit frugally chosen to slow the flow of scarce drachmas; and where is the town's small square, there is no answer in the passers-by for this universal stranger, the wandering Canaanite; I want to avoid it, if at least this once I didn't have to do it, the silence continues strewn around the town and I listen for and hear the bells that announce leprosy and when everyone moves away at hearing the sound, I approach the rotting flesh; an incomplete finger makes an effort to point: that way, northwards; I don't know why I ask, if the leper's answer is always the same, that way, northwards, I don't know why I ask if the square is always there, a few steps away; how beautiful today's square is, a central column made of marble which reaches up to the height of my solar plexus, the podium on which I rest my hand; and now the parchment that begins to grow, forming beneath my fingers, and hieroglyphic, cuneiform, alphabetic combinations that I trace with invisible, electric waves, that escape from my eyebrows, only because of this old impulse to give voice to the written word; I'm aware of the strength of my beard which has started to go a little grey, I'm aware of the vigour of my body; on each side of the podium loudspeakers of air begin forming to transmit the sound of my voice which will go on drawing the heads, bodies, tunics, sandals; the audience, child of my voice awaits my sound: "I have not come to speak of my sandals which transform themselves into buskins so that you can judge my height, the stars speak, the signs, Balthazar, Caspar, Melchior, will insist in the North star; Moses, Abraham, David in the Egyptian tower, I have known them all, do not believe in false stones, subduers of giants, do not believe in the one who is prepared to kill his son, do not believe in magic wands that refuse to bring forth springs of water; during the course of the years someone called Herod will want to asphyxiate the child that will cry; don't give him a name; he belongs to everyone, he is the all-child, he is the sob from your breast;" a whirlwind carries away my voice so that the heads begin to disappear, and the bodies, the tunics, the sandals; the square is left empty, my buskins fall apart and I am once again my normal height; the hieroglyphics vanish, the parchment turns to dust; the staff in my hand, and the usual joy in my breast: the fulfilment of my destiny as prophet; and now, at the setting of the sun, to set out for the desert, to occupy the desert night, to transform myself into an oasis so that the mouths of sand devour me

Peter the Long had carried his fame as a preacher with him; they had seen him, this they could affirm without room for error, Peter the Long travelled the face of the earth on foot, shod in espadrilles worn out with use, sandals whose soles had dissolved into the desert's hostile heat waves, so that he was frequently left with his bare feet covered with blisters and burns caused by the implacable sands; Peter the Long survived these marches that took him to the most remote points of the earth, thanks to his thick staff, of hard wood, on whose round head he rested the palm of his hand, he braced himself to alleviate the almost insufferable anguish caused by his tortured feet; on his journey through the towns, speculation and discussions by the inhabitants had defined the purpose of the staff with different results, these being the three most popular interpretations: Peter the Long used the staff as a symbol of the Authority of the Word; Peter the Long used the staff to help him and relieve him of the multiple blisters that tortured his feet on his long journeys; Peter the Long used the staff to defend himself from any impudent person who thought of assaulting him along the way; Peter believed that he had been born to deliver universal messages, but never to speak to every neighbour's son who might confront him to talk nonsense; as a result, upon his arrival at each new town, he went straight to a leper begging in the town square, because, as everyone knew, lepers were trained to be brief out of respect for the fear of infection that was felt by all; Peter insisted in approaching lepers although it had already been shown that they were not the best guides, confined, as they were, to a sector of the town which they left only to go to the square and carry out their profession as beggars, being ignorant of all other areas; Peter the Long, like all landowners, was a man of habit and repetition and, although unwillingly, did what no-one forced him to: approach, with a certain amount of apprehension, the first leper that he found and ask him questions that would help him choose a strategic site for his sermon, and quickly distance himself from the leper feeling annoyed and condescending at the same time; Peter the Long had arrived for the first time at the town of Chencho the Leper, inhabitant of a house made of palm leaves on the outskirts of the town, which was known as the little leprosy sanatorium because there, his wife and ten children formed a leper colony which, if it were not for fear of contagion, everyone would visit with frequency, being, as it was, a model of order and cleanliness; Chencho, a man who refused to live from public charity, had come up with an idea to start a portable business, a means of earning his daily bread without imitating those detestable blind men that exploited the generosity of their fellowmen, much like the exploitation practised -of this Chencho was certain- by other lepers that, according to news, conversations and verbiage, exist in other regions on the face of the earth; in this way the idea was born and gave rise in practise to the Chencho Industry, Specialized Monoproduct which was advertised in the big letters that appeared on the board: Melted Ices, Speciality of Chencho the Leper; a slogan that, although exaggerated in the plural, he had kept for its ring and effect; each morning the board was paraded around the square, carried in his hands or resting on Chencho's head; in the centre of the board was a paper cup that day after day became less white and which contained a little water with the exact dose of crimson aniline necessary to have it pass as a product derived from strawberries or the sapota, the latter also being known as mamey, for the proper and exigent regional linguistic adaptation; as stated in the slogan, the crimson water should be considered to be, what hours before had been a strawberry or sapota flavoured ice cube, and that now appeared in its liquid form owing, supposedly, to the presence of an unrelenting heat; the town's inhabitants, respecting the dignified posture of Chencho the Leper in not wishing to depend on the charity and generosity of his fellow man, approached the board and ordered a melted ice cube of strawberries or sapota, also called mamey; after ordering, the townsman paid Chencho the three *centavos* that the melted ice cube cost, inclined his head a little to one side to indicate that he had changed his mind and told Chencho that he could keep the melted ice cube because he had decided to go to the cafe on the corner, which at the time was already known as the Petit Miami, to have a Coca Cola like any neighbour's son who wanted to gain relief from the suffocating heat, with which Chencho's aim of trying not to abuse the generosity of his fellowman was satisfied; but one day it happened, as it does on those days when unfortunate things occur, that a matron, upon receiving the two *centavos* worth of change for the *medio* she had given, received a finger that without doubt belonged to Chencho and which had detached itself from him like that, without more ado, along with the copper ring recognizable as the wedding band that Chencho always wore; the matron, of about seventy years of age and dressed with dignity in a severe black suit, carefully deposited the finger on the board, next to the paper cup and retired with a silence somewhere between surprise and condescension; from that moment, his clients gave Chencho exactly three *centavos,* which they placed directly onto the board to pay for the Specialized Monoproduct, which itself seemed perhaps, as some had said, to be stuck to the surface of the board which was now full of *centavos,* orphaned for all time from the variety of coins that served it as ornamentation in the old days: *medios* of five *centavos, reales* of ten *centavos, pesetas* of twenty *centavos;* Peter the Long lost all notion of time, he did not know since when he had been on the rostrum that they had prepared for his Sermon, neither did he know when he had begun to speak; what he did know was that there, before him and with a look that he wished to classify as friendly but was forced to classify as aggressive, stood, in all the breadth and height of his stature, his honour the mayor whose voice did not delay: "in the name of the Municipal Committee we were going to permit you to read that parchment that you say was found in a cave and that speaks so well of the Jews; and know this once and for all, here it is said that you, however deep, deep-down, you may wish to hide it, are nothing more than a Jew, but well, well, we already know that this parchment deals with important points made by illustrious Jews that appear in the most respectable books of antiquity, and we are prepared, open as we are to all information that arrives at the doors of our beloved town, to listen to you with the proper respect that is owed to culture, but this business of doing conjurer's tricks, no, not that, as you are not Mandrake the Wizard nor have you come here for that type of swindle; with regard to the supposed hostility that you may interpret as emanating from us, I should tell you, and I insist on this, that they saw you produce a little paper which appeared from between your fingers, like magic, when the wind blew, and later, when it blew again and also as if by magic, you provided yourself with an audience so big that not one of the chairs we had brought here for the use of the inhabitants of our town was left vacant, loaned, as an act of civility, by our town council, along with other organizations, committees and schools prepared to cooperate for the good of the municipality, and it is only reasonable that, upset by this invasion of interlopers, they armed themselves with sticks and clubs to evict them from here, just as they deserve; and all this to end up feeling foolish because you deprived them, or more to the point, you deprived us all, of carrying out our civic duty, given that, when our citizens approached the interlopers and before they could touch them, you sent a gust of air and made them all vanish -the interlopers, that is- and in view of the fact that you have destroyed any possibility of showing our community spirit, we ask you, in the name of the Municipal Committee, that you be so good as to step down and move away from this place and these inhabitants who do not take kindly to your fooling them with magic tricks;" Peter the Long left the square, he paused a moment in what some interpreted as profound meditation and which was no more than a habit of remaining entranced, devouring with his eye sockets the space which one day would have to disappear; although, all things considered, he was the one who had to disappear in an unprecedented act of stopping the propagation, unstoppable up until now, of eternity, at least in him, Peter Matei, the Rebel of Time; without knowing how, he found himself accompanied and supported by his staff, on the road which would take him away from the town, without feeling in any part of his body, the gaze of Chencho the Leper, visible at the window of his house, from where he refrained from waving a goodbye that could jeopardize him as it would any neighbour's son who dared to exchange greetings with an undesirable; Peter Matei, nicknamed the Long, carried with him, despite everything, his sense of mission, the way and manifestation of the Authority of the Word, and without realising it, raised his voice to address an audience most definitively absent: "don't you listen to the holy words?" but, at the same time, he felt himself invaded by something diluted, diluting, that purified him so as to convert him into water, and something occurred which he would never confess to anyone: the obscure temptation to submerge himself, alone, in the immense vastness of the sand and from these depths, to hear himself shout: "inhospitable regulations, accelerated creche, lineal ebullience, whisper in disagreement, lateral pain, closed formol, vertical mind, overflowing rocky mountain, horizontal line, open-work embroidered dressing gown, ancestral song, recondite act, unusual dream almost eternal, eternal, eternal"

KA

the carrier of all weights, the bearer of so many responsibilities, the vizier, the principal delegate, the total representative, the one anointed with power, this is me, with my cloth of white linen putting distance between my skin and the air that surrounds me, without a haik, without a burnous, in this land of eyes in almond frames, blackened with alcohol dust, coloured in the green of malachite; the bearer of responsibilities, but also, this power that attends me as I cut the air with my indifference, with my hieratic progression, my smooth, shaven body, and all those I don't look at, sensing the touch of my power shaping my aura; the persistent security of my invulnerable position, my indifference to the Jews, why trouble myself to explore their condition as an oppressed people; there is a distant echo that seems to reach me, a voice that comes out of a past regression or which skips ahead to a projection yet to come, an echo which appears from an imprecise dimension, visions of a journey, sandals traversing paths to fulfil a destiny, I was indeed a descendent of Abraham and my voice anoints heads that form to listen to me; why linger over games of the imagination if everything is already there, my indifference towards the fingers that stretch out to me without reaching me, they all beg, they all complain, they all need, and I rush through my tribunals to be rid of them: yes, grant this piece of land to this one, no, don't delay the presentation of evidence and claims, I'm in a hurry, let's finish quickly; yes, condemn these three accused to anything, to death, to hard labour, to indefinite sentences, no, don't delay the presentation of evidence and claims, I'm in a hurry, let's finish quickly; yes, take on the vigilance of Sirius which threatens to cause the Nile to flood again, and if there are dangers, let the delegates take the necessary measures, or are you not, perhaps, even capable of defending yourselves against water? yes, approve this will as it stands, deny the claims of the presumptive heirs that arrived from Nubia, don't delay the presentation of evidence, I'm in a hurry, let's finish quickly; no, it doesn't matter who came to intercede for the Jews, I didn't care yesterday, and I will not have anything to do with them tomorrow either; today's appeals are closed, tell the scribe to leave, all of you leave, I will reconvene this tribunal tomorrow, this domain of formulae that I manipulate just to get by; and now, to leave this place behind, to go in search of my vocation; yes, it is comfortable to relax in this power, to manipulate the exercise of my will without others manipulating me, but how to get the King-God to allow me to encounter my destiny; audience with Ramses II, yes, allowed, and today, again, it is my turn to listen, always listen, the fight with the Hittites, the monuments, look, vizier, projects for more and more monuments; monuments with my effigy as King-God repeated on the colossi of Abu Simbel, guardians of the Nile, to leave on the walls the memory of all my great deeds, the Kadesh victory, my cartouche engraved in existing monuments so as to leave in them my mark, projects for monuments, grand vizier, always monuments; and when it is my turn to speak, now my intention to almost demand, with almost urgency, comes out like a restrained repetition which the King-God hears without giving importance, without giving a definite answer, without giving; I leave, conscious of the mistaken role I have been given to live out in this dynasty, I'm conscious of everything, my hieratic walk, the eyes in frames blackened with alcohol dust, the women maintaining their elegance in the kalasiris, and at my approach, let everyone move aside, let them retract their outstretched hands that never tire of begging; now I am moving towards my vocation, towards the destiny that Ramses will one day concede to me: to preserve his body, to be the absolute guardian of his Ka, to leave my indestructible craftsmanship in the river of the centuries, Ramses's mummy; I approach the embalmer's shop, I want to practise, to practise incessantly, I have watched him practising for years on less important bodies seeking the perfection of the mummification destined for Ramses; and always, the same attitude of the embalmer at my presence, he looks at me as though he were seeing a mad dreamer, but he doesn't dare disobey, and I read the uneasiness in his eyes: I haven't even taken time to choose my mastaba, why does this mummification obsess me so; when I read the question in his eyes, I mutter something to deflect his suspicion: interest in mummification is an interest just like any other, like one might have in sculpture; the embalmer looks away and only speaks because it is necessary to explain the process to me: we have a new, intact cadaver, it has just arrived; he uncovers for me, laid out, the nude body of a young man and begins removing his brain through a recently made cavity; on the right flank, a rapid incision through which deft hands begin removing the entrails, one by one, leaving the heart; the entrails will be placed in the four canopic jars; the empty cavity is carefully washed; I insist that the embalmer allows me to arrange the cadaver in the enormous receptacle which contains a solution of salt or natron where it must remain for several weeks until the fat is drained; I also insist that he allows me to remove the other cadaver that is now ready, from the large container where it left its fat in the solution of salt or natron; this time I don't allow him to skin the cadaver: I must be the one to pull all the skin from the body, leaving the skin on the head which has not been submerged in the solution, and I insist that in the days to follow I must finish the mummification process; my attention is drawn to the nails on the feet and hands, tied on with wire, and upon filling the cranium and the cavity, empty of entrails, with preservatives, I am invaded, for the first time, by the fulfilment of my mission, the gods have destined me to preserve for all time the body of Ramses; the voice of the embalmer pulls me from my fantasy: we must cover the cadaver with a paste of resin and fat, then we will start with the bandages; upon leaving the shop where I feel so close to my destiny as embalmer, doubts assail me, the embalmer is tricking me, he is training me in false methods so that Ramses, when the moment arrives, will consider me incapable of his eternal glorification; my aspiration to perpetuate the figure of Ramses remains, and more, to officiate in every way, to be responsible for the ceremony of opening the mouth, the ears, the eyes so that for all eternity the mummy of Ramses can absorb sustenance, can hear and see everything; to invoke the use of his organs and with amulets and litanies, stimulate the heart, the dorsal spine, the blood, to officiate at the funeral banquet which will serve as sustenance for his mummy, to watch over his Ka; but when I speak to Ramses: I sense that I will discover the perfect mummification formula, I could be... I could...; Ramses doesn't hear me, his conversation revolves around Abu Simbel, and his treatment of me is always that which he would accord the grand vizier, I leave the King-God thinking that I will only ever be that to him, the vizier; if no-one knows my secret, how can the embalmer know it, why would he trick me with false procedures, or perhaps the embalmer has intuited that which Ramses could never intuit, this irreplaceable course; it would be best to surprise him, suddenly appear in the shop when he is not expecting me, today, right now when he knows me to be at the tribunal, today is the moment, now, and I hear my voice: all audiences are hereby cancelled; I head for the shop with firm steps, controlling my breathing so as to have enough air; the embalmer doesn't dare protest; I am aware of the discomfort my presence causes him; he resigns himself, takes me to the cadaver of an eleven year old child, and upon seeing it, I attempt to control my rage; this is not a fresh cadaver; you have already treated it, the process is different, you have left the skin intact, what have you done, tell me what you have done, you have been teaching me false methods; the embalmer, without raising his eyes, as if preparing himself to work intensively on the cadaver, confined himself to say: this is not yet a new method, it's an attempt, a treatment with poisonous resins, a treatment that I have yet to perfect; his voice seems sincere, but I remain sceptical; I order him out of the shop and there I stay, standing before the laid out cadaver of the child, his skin discoloured, slippery, how many days, how many weeks has he been dead, something keeps me there, absorbed, invaded by that vision, in the space of the whole universe that is emptied so that this cadaver and I can occupy it, possessing each other so powerfully that any other living -or deceased- person is eradicated, everything becomes distant, only this cadaver here, just as the cadaver of Ramses could be alone with my presence as officiator of all the ceremonies, it would not be enough for me to be Ramses's perpetuator; Ramses should inhabit me, Ramses must live in me; I'm aware of the sharp instrument in my hand and the thin strip of flesh that I tear from the cadaver to devour with one quick movement; my legs buckle... why are my legs folding... the dull noise that my body makes seems alien to me as I fall, and the voice of the embalmer reaches me from afar: the vizier, the grand vizier has died it was election time in that so aptly named Guaso Town: "Chicho Bota for Councilman;" posters with Chicho's large face were on all the telephone poles, on all the columns of public and private buildings, on all the walls of buildings with prime location; Chicho's enormous face multiplied and accosted one even in the Bonilla Pharmacy, the Montecarlo Café, the Petit Miami, the Current Affairs Cinema, the Faust Cinema, the America Bar, the Venus Hotel -with its dubious reputation-, the Spanish Colony, Ricardo's Printing Services, and in this way pursuing one as far as the Market Square; Peter the Long well remembers this multiplication, this invasion, and the presence of Chicho Bota for he was the one responsible for pasting the posters and for choosing the strategic spots from which Chicho Bota's immobile eyes seemed to watch every passer-by as if willing them to approve of the slogan he himself had invented to cover his poster; at its head, across the photo of his enormous face, were the black, jet black letters: "Chicho Bota for Councilman," and at the foot of the photo, "Exemplary Citizen of Guaso Town;" Peter the Long looks back at this time and remembers himself as being young, very young, although everyone knows that he was never young, just as it is common knowledge that he travelled tirelessly in search of the secret formulas of the Word, inventing numerous litanies that would transport him to eternal oblivion while, naturally, leaving his mark on the world; leaving behind, it goes without saying, a creation which would, for ever and ever, ensure that his name, the name of Peter, nicknamed the Long, live on as a vertical echo crossing the centuries; being made Chicho Bota's publicity officer was not enough, nor was Peter satisfied with the important task entrusted to him by Chicho Bota: that of attending to all, or almost all, those who arrived at his offices to ask the future Councilman for favours in advance; it was Peter the Long's job to decide which petitions would be considered and which ignored; Peter the Long paced the town with great strides attempting, during these hikes, to find the right words with which to confront Chicho: "let me preserve your effigy for ever in the form of your own body, draw up a legal document saying that, as your last will and testament, you grant me the privilege of embalming you; by then I'll have found the perfect method and you'll remain intact and exact, as if you were alive; standing, dressed in knight's armour, you will preside over our City Hall for all eternity; my name, Peter the Long, will appear on a small plaque located near your right foot;" these carefully chosen words were never to reach the ears of Chicho Bota, concerned, as he always was, with other forms of permanence which, at the time, seemed to him to be more appropriate and effective: the huge posters bearing his face and the words that defined him; on hundreds of occasions Peter the Long was observed standing before Chicho Bota with these words on the tip of his tongue, but each time the same thing happened; "you, Peter, attend to the posters and keep these people happy so that they vote for me, but without promising them too much;" Peter continued to stride about town with a gait that became distressing; he followed a circular route which he repeated day in and day out until the inevitable happened:

Peter the Long went towards the outskirts of town, he passed the cemetery and continued walking for a long time; the sun beat down on his forehead making him sweat; when exhaustion began to invade his body he found himself at his destination, standing before Tuntún the black, an old, lottery ticket vendor reputed to be a shaman and well versed, so they said, in the art of embalming small birds and tortoises; both entered the hut with its interior dimly lit owing to a lack of electricity; the stump of a candle illuminated the session; following a round of intense sucking, turning and chewing on its damp end, the cigar butt clamped between the thick lips of the black man began to emit a curtain of smoke through its reddened ashes; the transformation began, accompanied by what appeared to be a long swallow of rum; Tuntún became Changuito and related this transformation in his africanized Cuban: I Changuito, you know? I son of Saint Bálbala as them call in Christian language the African god Changó, you know, my son? I horse ridden by dead one who is going to tell you everything, everthing, my son, you know? Changuito horse speak with African Cuban tongue, you unnastand me, my son? sssussssusss! you be famous as you like with this balming, heeey! heeey! sssussssusss! start balming with birdie, must pass birdie through body and then start balming; you be famous heeey! heeey! sssussssusss! I give herbs for you, for you do balming, you stand me, my son? Changuito horse give herbs for you; I not say how you do balming, you stand me, my son? cause balming business your business, my son; Changuito horse only give herbs cause the dead one does not say how you do balming but you be famous because famousness is here, with us, dead one says that famousness is at your foot, at your two feets, my son; heeey! heeey! sssussssusss!"   old Tuntún regained his composure as if, moments before, he had not contorted himself, as if, moments before, he had not spoken in tongues nor been the dead one's horse; he stretched, extending his arms as if he had just woken out of a long, deep sleep, behaving with the calm and satisfaction of one who is in possession of all the world's truths; he asked his new client, who had said he was called Peter Matei, how it had gone during the consultation because he, Tuntún, knew nothing of what Changuito said or did when ridden by the dead one; he only knew that he should give Peter a small Australian bird which had just been caught in one of the small cages used for trapping birds and affirmed that he could guarantee that any ritual that he performed using the little bird would bring him success because it was well looked after and must have come from some rich house that had patios full of elegant cages full of exorbitantly expensive birds and that this one, in an unguarded moment, must have escaped and that he, Tuntún, must charge him five pesos which included the consultation, the directions for the ritual and which, with bird and everything, was a bargain and the only reason he charged anything was because the dead ones insisted and this was the amount they required, five pesos; Peter Matei, unaccustomed as he was to hearing tongues spoken and not knowing anything about these rituals, was speechless when Tuntún asked him in whose name Changuito had said the work should be carried out, if it was in the name of Ochún, of Changó, of the Seven Powers, of Obatalá or of Eleguá, and when confronted with Peter's surprised silence, Tuntún concluded by saying that if Changuito had not given any instructions in this regard, that he should carry out the ritual in the name of whomsoever inspired him; Peter Matei, unaccustomed as he was to the works of the *babalaos* understood that the little bird had to be inside his body in order for the ritual or work, as the old black man Tuntún called it, to have the desired effect, and decided to carry out this ritual in the name of that eternity in which he had decided not to participate; Peter locked himself in one of Chicho Bota's offices and, believing that he was following the ritual to the letter, held the parakeet to each part and corner of his body, at the end of which, the parakeet gave him a strange look and decided to choose that moment to die; Peter the Long bathed the small body in the now cool water in which he had already boiled the herbs and, without giving it much thought, opened his mouth and swallowed the bird - beak, feathers and all - as quickly as possible while, at the same time, asking himself how this contact between feathers and skin, herb bath and final swallowing was going to make him famous, and how this was going to prepare the way for him to preserve for posterity the body of Chicho Bota in its suit of armour, so that it could preside over the Guaso Town's City Hall; he had not quite finished examining these possibilities when he was overcome by a strange lightness which lead, most definitively, into a fainting spell from which he was able to hear in the distance: "it's Peter, come quick, Peter the Long has fainted;" Peter regained consciousness in the First Aid Clinic to discover that he had scandalized the town with what was considered to be a strange type of suicide attempt involving swallowing a bird soaked in aniline solution which, everyone knows, is poisonous and which was present, impregnating the feathers, despite the herb bath; this incident cost Changuito a large part of his clientele because, and quite rightly so, a son of Changó does not tell anyone to swallow whole birds, or anything else for that matter, which have been soaked in aniline solution; this incident also cost Peter the Long his position as publicity officer to the future Councilman Chicho Bota, a post which, all things considered, in no way interested Peter because his true vocation was that of tireless traveller and searcher for the formula to end eternity; during his rapid convalescence he walked to every corner of Guaso Town; today was Sunday and at eleven o'clock in the morning a fresh breeze wandered through the sunny surroundings; Peter the Long was walking along Crombet Street when suddenly, upon reaching Martí Park, he decided to cross the street, leaving behind the sidewalk he had been following to walk along the opposite side of the street; while crossing he took a few strides and when lifting his right leg for the third time, found himself in the streets of Manhattan, when he was most definitely a woman and where it was many, many years later, so many years later that it could even have been the year 1976, and the streets of Manhattan seemed an offensive grey without you, Chachita, as if they had skipped ahead to the end, to my death, without consulting me; losses, Chachi, are felt prematurely through premonitions, that's how the palmist put it and that was how I said it to you, Chachita, in that Swiss restaurant in Westchester and the news caused you pain and I also hurt because it was a loss that announced itself at an inopportune moment, far too soon for the two of us; in the dimness of the restaurant we loved each other deeply, Chachita, and we were solemn throughout dinner, almost solemn, between fearing that it would all end and taking refuge in our togetherness; it would all end after five or ten years had passed since our first meeting, and when I said, to cheer us up a little, that there were still at least four years to go, you sighed with sadness, Chachi; in spite of that moment which united us so profoundly, a few months later I began to feel the presence of a slow truth and it was, Chachita, what I think can be described as your indifference and I began to ask myself, Chachi, why we must suffer warnings and dreams until we find ourselves in a state of complete and irreversible isolation, made old by anticipation? your love, Chachi, the love you sang to me in so many poems, was to my bewilderment becoming a strange attachment; and guess what, Chachi, I even had a dream that reaffirmed all the palmist's premonitions and when I went to write it down in my diary, exactly as I'm telling it to you now that you are so far away that I don't even know if you are anywhere, when I went to write about it, as I was telling you, what I wrote was: I want to sleep in white, sleep only in white and switch off everything; Peter the Long felt his foot fall heavily on the other sidewalk and he continued striding forward in the direction of the river; he made himself comfortable under the bridge and began a litany with which he was sure he would, little by little and step by step, reach total oblivion: "devout lark, mellifluous serpentine, stiff dragonfly, engraved poet, anguished bravado, miserable opposition, organic naturalness, unexpected violence, glittering waterfall, burning jump, constant kiss, gregarious tripod, dusty millennium, numb consumer, dancing toad, nocturnal firefly, meddlesome butterfly, ancestral box, the joker, blushing path, lymphatic contamination, perverted fatigue, mischievous tendon, miserable opposition, miserable, miserable, miserable" and it was deep into the night when Peter the Long awoke briefly and slowly recognized the bridge, the moon was still up, incredibly bright, and he was still there; to avoid falling into a depression he held onto what he called a word talisman: "a stumble is not a fall and is even less a definitive fall"

THE GALLEYS

we have just left Alexandria, they say that this voyage ends at
the Port of Said; a short voyage, a long voyage, there is always
the sea, the journey, the rowing, rowing the galley; I allow
myself to be rocked by the rhythm which induces in me a state
of ecstasy so that my eyes glaze over and I can break through
reality's solid borders and soar to that ever-so crystalline realm;
the flight seems short when I confront myself with this generic
name to which I answer: Slave, the slave from Said, just another
possession belonging to the Pharaoh who makes me ride the
Mediterranean swells on an interminable voyage; and what
if I were born in China? I would be Mui Tsai and my poor
parents would have sold me to rich masters to use me as they
wished; and if I had been born amongst the pyramids, as free
as a bird? I would have grown like the wind until the moment
when I would find myself sentenced to the galleys for a crime I
committed, for a crime I did not commit, to forever touch this
driven wood which has put down roots in my hands; and in the
XI century? would I arrive in time to record the words of Saint
Thomas Aquinas at the moment when he declares that slavery
is the inescapable consequence of original sin and if I wait...?
if I wait I shall be born in the Congo to cross the Tropic of

Cancer to the New World, wrapped in my chains, in the chains that will always be a part of me like some calloused appendage of my skin; and what's the point of these questions if I have already learnt to forget myself, if I am now learning not to ask in which hemisphere my parents are living out their slavery just as I endure mine; now is the time to shatter the image that visits me occasionally, the image of the powerful man I once was when I used to force a path through the crowd with their arms outstretched; because it is now my lot to journey towards my death while sensing the crust of salt which searches for my cupped palms to open them to the mystery that I bury every day in the wood everybody said that Peter the Long was a crazy old man of no fixed abode but, at the same time, everyone contradicted themselves and declared that Peter the Long had never been a crazy old man; the one thing they did agree on was the part about no fixed abode because he was seldom seen doing anything other than walking; at times he walked with a camel-like quickness, trying desperately to eat up the distance that separated him from the river and where, under the bridge or on top of the huge boulder, he acquired his reputation for insanity, as the beggars that prowled the area, whether they came from Guaso Town or other points of the region, had repeatedly heard him sprouting nonsense, out loud, and often with his arms extended and his eyes rolled back, gibberish - they all agreed- which had neither beginning nor end; who was the old man insulting? who was he imploring? what was the purpose of these crazy remarks which sometimes took the form of a litany and at others were nothing more than profanities which appeared at any time of day to disturb the beggars' sleep while they were attempting to sleep in peace alongside the Guaso River, like any neighbour's son? but later, as if nothing had happened, Peter the Long covered kilometres, retracing his steps, following the same circuit, always alone except when he was carrying out some little chore which, as they said, he could perform just like any neighbour's son and, given that Peter the Long never bothered anyone, it was said that he was most definitely not crazy, but when Saturday arrived, the day the beggars went from door to door in the hopes of receiving a few coins and a chunk of stale bread, they also came with their stories about the old man, his litanies and his filthy words; four pasty, gelatinous women who had a cherry tree in their courtyard, waited anxiously for Saturday to arrive so that the black man, Musaraña, could tell them of the life and miracles of Peter the Long which, all things considered, were nothing more than a tangle of words and frequently, of four letter words; one particular Saturday, the four gelatinous women stationed themselves on the porch very early to await Musaraña, the beggar, who would tell them of Peter's latest verbal adventures; finally they spotted Musaraña approaching, squinting, grimacing and waving his hands as if he were clutching at invisible things in the empty air; on this particular day, the gelatinous women gave him three coins (two small, silvery Cuban coins and one American coin, much bigger and darker); and upon hearing him protest, only three lil' cents? they decided to make him happy by offering him a little hot chocolate in a rather old, rusty, tin can; the stale bread found a home in a dirty cloth in which it would stay wrapped until such time as hunger decided otherwise; Musaraña was standing next to the cherry tree, unable to appreciate its sweet scent because the overpowering odour of old urine which impregnated his rags had conquered the air; having downed the hot chocolate in a few gulps, Musa prepared to repeat Peter the Long's latest outburst which had occurred during the middle of the night and which Musa swore "by this", making a cross with his thumb and forefinger, was an exact imitation of what Peter the Long had said, all of it correctly pronounced, just as it had been pronounced by Peter: "I'm going to pee like an ugly dog and like a sulphurous devil, those men who used to cross the river would say with fury dripping from their teeth while drooling at the mouth: today our balls are excited; the thing is to fuck around and to fuck and fuck until your balls drop off because man is a never-ending dialogue in which he passes judgement and is judged, condemns, sets free, vomits, vomits, and vomits out unreality, time and time again, until it slowly becomes his own reality, exclusive, sad, involuntarily humorous, always seeped with the sweat of that which is infinite, inward looking infinity, like the shaft of the well: let the dogs collect all their mange and then you will see the rape of the cockroaches;" the four gelatinous women felt surprise take possession of their bland faces, it even made itself at home in their eyes, because what they had just heard was no prayer; one of those so-called intelligent people had said that Peter the Long recited litanies, but what Musaraña had just repeated was no litany because litanies are prayers that are said as part of the Hail Mary, and the four were well aware of this because they had attended, night after night, the seven o'clock mass; Peter the Long walked to the station to catch the train that would take him, jolting all the way, to Caimanera; during the twenty kilometre journey he had become so absorbed in looking out the window it was as if he wished to devour the view, interrupted as it was by telephone poles which flashed past; nothing but trees, dry-looking ground, and those maguey shrubs which he considered to be, for some inexplicable reason, a true mystery and, as always, his curiosity was aroused when they arrived at Novaliche, at that solitary mansion in the middle of nowhere that he always ended up scrutinizing during that stop; later, he was affected by the melancholy of the salt pan with its enormous rectangles which, to Peter's way of thinking, were breeding grounds for salt; while passing by Cemetery Hill, as it was called because the cemetery was located on a hill on the outskirts of Caimanera, the train decreased speed and Peter the Long was on the point of jumping down, or more to the point, of carefully throwing himself out in order to take a closer look at the area and of attempting to prove, by relating the fact to the site, whether the area had been the scene of the crime committed by Agachao only a few days previously or, at least, that's what they said: that they had seen Agachao carrying, on his back, a jute sack which appeared to be very heavy and which must surely contain the chopped up body of the man he had stabbed to death in order to steal the thousand pesos the man carried in his pocket; but the fact remained that Agachao was still on the loose, that he had not been apprehended, because, according to some, there was not enough proof that the money Agachao was suddenly able to squander was the stolen money, just as there was no proof that the jute sack that Agachao had been carrying was the self-same sack that had been found near the cemetery containing the remains of a dissected man; it was also said that what was happening was that everyone was scared of Agachao, who was a skinny man with the face of a felon and who always bent forward as if his spine had broken in the area of his cervix or dorsal vertebrae, and this made him form a right angle with his body; Peter the Long overcame the impulse to jump off the train because the sight of the cemetery hypnotized him making him give up his original intention of investigating the crime; upon leaving the train at Caimanera's old station he bought some plantain chips and some codfish fritters that are cooked in the portable, improvised stoves which proliferated in the small area demarcated by the station and the wharf, and on which the crowd thronged, moving between the launches and the train; before heading for the wharf where

Quintín always left him his little boat, without ever charging him for its use, Peter the Long ran the few steps to the restaurant owned by the Chinese and bought a slice of coconut pie and a slice of lemon pie which he would save for when hunger assailed him during the night; he was already on his way to untie the boat when he decided to head for the Islander's stand for an ultra strong cup of espresso, the kind they called *carretero;* once in the boat, with his hands on the paddle, he paddles a few strokes backwards and then lines the boat up in the direction of Boquerón; the sea was a little choppy and the sharks were about, across the length and breadth of the bay; from time to time Peter the Long stopped paddling to bail out the boat, scooping out the water with a dirty, chipped, pewter jug; almost at Boquerón, perhaps because of the tension caused by the danger, he found that he had gone quite rigid, his hands aching, because not having found a formula to end eternity it worried him to die just to continue living on in another form; it was already dark when he chose his spot to fish for lobsters; it would have been easier to row along the Caimanera coastline up to Nunque, to catch little fish called *manjúas* with a net like the one used for catching butterflies, because, as Quintín said, the boat was no longer fit to ride the high seas; there was something in that heartrending solitude that made him return, time after time, to the same spot; once settled in his patch of water, Peter threw the lobster pots overboard and focused the light that illuminated the transparent water; Peter the Long became hypnotized by the light that sank towards the depths of the sea; remaining immobile caused him to feel invaded by an anguish of waiting that soon became interminable; yes, Chachita, I can hear you fine, where are you calling from, Grand Central? and why are you crying Chachi? because you missed the train? that was how I questioned you, Chachi, one question after another;

I was desperately asking you questions because you don't know, Chachi, the anguish it caused me to hear you cry, I just didn't know what to do nor where to put myself and that's why I suggested to you that you take the express that stopped at the next station, the one after Scarborough, because when I heard you cry I quickly looked up the itinerary and told you to take the train that would leave from Grand Central Station in a few minutes so that you would not have to wait there for so long and so that you would stop crying, but I tell you, when I suggested this I was afraid because the other station is dangerous, Chachi, people are assaulted and robbed and other crimes occur there, that's why I went to wait for you, well in advance, so that you wouldn't feel all alone in that place where not even taxis will go and while I waited for you I became more and more frightened until my heart was beating like crazy when three cars full of Blacks appeared and began to drive in circles around me and I, just imagine, Chachi, how frightened I was because as you know, the lock on the right door of the Plymouth was broken and wouldn't close properly, but I stayed put and I continued to feel an ever increasing fear, overpoweringly so, until the train arrived and the three cars disappeared; but as you can see, Chachita, even afraid and everything, I stayed there to wait for you, so that you wouldn't be alone; as frightened as I was I stayed, Chachi, just to wait for you, even though I never told you this; the next day we went cycling; and I, riding slowly but without feeling hampered by the slowness of the Huffy that you had given me, because the truth is, I felt well-and-truly free riding bicycles with you; although sometimes I would say, Chachi, and I don't know if you remember this, that the Huffy took me, not where I wanted to go, but where she felt like going, and I told you playfully that this bicycle had a mind of her own, but what I should have said and what I'm saying now that I don't even know where you are, Chachi, is that I was always falling off, although I don't know what was wrong with me because when I was a little girl I rode a bicycle so well, really well, and later, as you know, Chachi, I was always sprawled on the ground, I would see you on your yellow bicycle, pedalling away as if it were easy, and me behind, on the Huffy that was so black and so slow and I often thought, I'm going to fall, but I kept on pedalling and pedalling, just to keep up with you Chachita, just to follow you and if I fell, I knew that you would laugh with that affection that I found so appealing and that would stay with me; I swear, Chachi, even if I never told you so; with the first rays of dawn, Peter the Long pulled the still empty lobster pots from the water and headed for the coast, paddling

A CYCLE AWAY

they called it the Enclave, that area enclosed with barbed wire and surrounded by the remains of a military base crawling with refugees who brought with them, in them, a small piece of hell stuck to their skin, like a habit; stabbings, thefts, lies, pain, loss of liberty, suffocation, human misery; in the cubicle in which I had to interview refugees, it may have been the month of October, any day of the week: what prison were you at, how many years were you in jail, which psychiatric hospital were you released from, and you, did you choose to come to this country? "no, they made me, they put me on a ship that sailed out of Mariel, and I, I would have chosen to remain in EL Combinado because, even though they sentenced me to twenty years, at least my family are in Cuba;" yes, it was October and it could have been any day of the week; the cubicle was empty of voices; I became very aware of myself, of my body sitting on that chair with wheels that buried itself in the hollow under the desk; I inclined my head, hid my face in my arms and a vision from another dimension began opening itself up to me; I recognised the power of my eyes, I knew that sight has another purpose, but I didn't immediately understand the meaning of this vision; one month later I left the Enclave; by plane, from Fort Smith, I crossed several states, heading North East; I arrived at those familiar streets and walked them once again; an unseen guide directed my steps to those halls permeated with the smoke of incense, inhabited by women swathed in white saris who moved with ethereal grace and made of dawn a time for meditation; at times of learning I heard your voice, beautiful yogi, that came to touch the space with its magic and to bring our golden age back to our memories; at dawn your look brought us light; when your eyes gazed deeply into mine, I understood the meaning of my first vision; I knew that our histories had touched, skin to skin, in other incarnations, I also knew that we had been born in a perfect land, a cycle away, where wisdom, light and love predominated, where divisions according to gender did not exist, nor kingdoms, nor properties; where we spent our time working for the common good, carrying out our duties to the best of our abilities, making the most of our aptitudes and, during periods of recreation, we went out into the clean air of the valleys on long hikes, till dusk; it was a land with universal inhabitants, bathed in a benevolent golden light through which we communicated in silence; you and I recognised our origins in our parents' eyes, and we watched other beings of light emerge from our own eyes to disperse throughout the universe carrying the message in Guaso Town the news spread like wildfire: Peter Matei had become a Mason, he had been seen in the yard of the Caimanera Lodge although no-one could ascertain whether it was at a time when the Lodge brothers normally met or whether the Lodge had been deserted, but he had definitely been there, with apron and everything, in a state of agitation, alone, in that yard, pulling faces, standing upright, and with his hands pressed together as if he were about to pray; they say that he stayed like that for several hours, grimacing and with his hands together in prayer until, suddenly, he began yelling, at the top of his voice and loud enough to wake the dead, as if to hurl insults at someone who had interrupted him: "really, Rodrigo, why cause that deafening sound at this hour? well, man, it doesn't matter what time it is, this business of going around shooting cannons is enough to drive anyone crazy, ahhhh! that land, land? so it was first called Guanahaní and then San Salvador? if it is land, land, well fuck the land;" the eyes that watched him from the backyard affirmed that Peter the Long calmed himself in due course and then, concentrating intensely, began to recite a litany: "nosy eye, small aluminium intestinal wind, multiple brick, horizontal encyclopedia, categoric auction, slanderous kite, dissolved punishment, voracious tape recorder, disgraced seed, glorious ostrich body, restless horizon, true skylight, redeemed corner, vertical launch, canned madrigals, starch torches, debated molars, calamari from the South, arterial kidneys, lung improvement, vertebral doves, riding boncs, colossal horseman, categoric auction, horizontal, voracious, voracious, voracious"; the comments flew in this hotbed of scandal and even the town priest felt obliged to make a general and emphatic announcement that arrived, like a thunderclap dressed in kindness, immediately after the sermon when, without any preamble or explanation, he stated most forcefully that all Masons were headed directly for hell and that all the people there present knew to what he was referring and that he preferred to say nothing more on the subject of that secret society, in which the devil was surely involved, out of respect for the place in which he found himself at that moment and, without further ado, he got down from the pulpit leaving behind a nervous congregation impatient to add this new occurrence, that of the priest's intervention, to the many comments that had already been made; with mass over the congregation gathered in the park where they crowded around the statues of heroes and, to their surprise, discovered that they all agreed that in no way did they want Peter the Long to head straight for hell and that they doubted he would because they did not believe him capable of joining hidden societies like this one, at the end of which, one of the group felt brave enough to say aloud to another, so that the others could overhear him: "no, my friend, I know Matei, what reason does he have to become a Mason; yes, alright, I have been told that Masons wear little aprons, but if they saw Matei wearing an apron it must have been because he was going to sweep the yard of the Lodge; friend, Peter is just a poor wretch, a poor devil that would have gone there to sweep in order to make a living, and those things he was saying there in the yard, that barrage of talk, I assure you that had nothing to do with the Lodge, it was just one of those strange things he does, because maybe what they say is true, that he's half round the bend;" as the days went by the mood calmed and the debates and the comments lessened, although it is true that there were still a few boys lagging behind who approached him to poke fun at him: "so, Peter, you're looking for something in the mysteries? listen, be careful, this is not good for your spirit, and even less so for your head;" but Peter never answered them because, as always, he remained absorbed in his own world; yes, of course I remember, Chachita, that the day before I left for Fort Chaffee to interview refugees I spent the whole day pacing the apartment, choosing bits and pieces from here and there that I wanted to put in the suitcases that you were going to pack for me, and I also spent the day making jokes and laughing all the time while wearing a little hat like the one Rex Harrison wore in *My Fair Lady;* and when I called you from Fort Chaffee from a public phone, feeling so desolate in the pitch dark, when you heard my voice you started to cry, Chachi, even though I had told you nothing of the desolation of that call box from which I was phoning you, and I asked you, sounding as brave as I knew how, but what's the matter, Chachita, there's no reason to cry, I'm fine here, just fine; and you told me it was because of the little hat, that you remembered how I spent the whole day wandering around with that hat on my head; and, Chachita, I think you know too that when I play the fool and laugh, it's to chase away the fear of becoming miserable; I think you know this, Chachi, even though you have never said so; that year I went from one strange experience to the next; as if I were on another planet where everything was so sad and desolate; and when the Cuban woman who stayed in the same barracks I did said to me, "I'm going to need you soon because Myrna's leaving and I don't know if I can bear the sadness," I replied that, yes, I would keep her company, and when Myrna left, the woman came to see me everyday to tell me how unhappy she was and one day she told me that she was an alcoholic and if she became too miserable, she was going to start getting drunk again, and on another day she invited me to spend a weekend in Eureka Springs and in the guesthouse she asked for a double bed and I said that two singles would be better, because I could see then that her yearning for Myrna needed another type of comfort, and she was drinking too much, and when we returned to the base, I suggested we go for walks at night to see if, in this way, she might forget about drinking, even if only for a little while, but even while walking she drank her beers and one night, in my room, she got into my bed and we allowed ourselves to wake up together so as to ease our despair a little, because that is a place, Chachita, where one can die for want of a dream, and that's why, when this woman left, I built my dreams around a tall, blonde American woman, just as, one year before in Westchester, I had fantasized about the Chilean woman who was passing through, but you already know all this, Chachita, because I told you everything; I always yearned for you because you were part of where I came from, of me, of everything that I touched, just as I was a part of who you were and that's what you used to say to me, "come, come soon because this apartment just isn't home without you, because the warmth is missing;" but I couldn't leave because it was too difficult to find work and I wanted to save some money so that later on we would lack nothing and that's why, when you said that you had bought a stereo, that you wanted us to take a trip to Mexico to attend a conference and that you had painted the apartment, that's why I scolded you on the phone and you cried because you had painted the apartment with such love, and after I had spoken to you, I cried for a long time and I'm crying now, Chachi, that I don't know where you are or even if you are anywhere, because I cannot forgive myself for that; but yes, I did leave when I heard you say that you were going to India with a group of female Yogis, to Mount Abu, where great things were going to happen and I was afraid that you would stay there, believing that you had found the path that you often thought you had found, when you locked yourself in the room where your desk was, to carry out your ceremonies and secret rituals, as if you were looking for the key with which to uncover mysteries; and while it is true that I would always have longed for you, if I had known that you had found your path, I would have felt a sad and lonely resignation, but not knowing what you were getting into, no, not that, Chachita, I would not have been able to live knowing that you were feeling sad and alienated in some far off place, and I, without any word from you, Chachi, never again to hear your voice; upon my return, almost immediately, we moved nearer, closer to Manhattan, because from Sunnyside it was so easy to get to the Yoga Centre, do you remember, Chachi? and I soon got used to vegetarian food and to practising celibacy with you, because you said that we had to remain pure, but for me, remaining celibate with you was nothing new, because it started almost immediately during your first visits to Westchester, when you wanted nothing to do with anything sexual, and it was all so strange, Chachi, because when you weren't there with me it was as if your life were meaningless and the same thing happened to me and we shared a profound intimacy, used the language lovers have and shared a feeling of home that you created; these contradictions within one and the same situation that seemed so stable, made me write things in my diary that, at the time, I didn't understand as I do now, Chachi, that you are so far away that I don't even know if you are anywhere at all; at the time I told myself that all questions fired at the future would become an answerless echo but, meanwhile, we would continue to share the thermos of coffee I prepared for you at six in the morning, the occasional book that would arrive, so many types of affection; if you are somewhere, Chachita, and if you can hear me, then you must understand that it wasn't easy to unravel this, because I have your letters that for the first time in so long I'm re-reading, and it is difficult to believe that the great love they contain is nothing more than a strange form of affection; and for this, perhaps for this, I spent the first five years thinking only of you, until suddenly I felt the need to fantasize, to meet someone that I could dream about; because, for me, this was now becoming embarrassing and very difficult, when at times you told me that you felt guilty for not giving me what I needed and I told you that it was okay, because what was happening to me, and this I swear to you, was that I myself chose another direction and when I was visited by an attack of passion, I erased your image and I embraced someone I had made-up or perhaps remembered, so that the fear would not be let loose in me, the fear that you would want to banish me forever, that you would want to run away from me, that you would want to avoid me, but I never realised this until now, when I don't even know where you are; there in Westchester I never stopped to decipher the control I subjected myself to, an iron control, a shield to protect myself from fear until I began to believe, Chachi, that it wasn't for you, that it was for someone invented or perhaps remembered, or borrowed from a reality that was not mine, but you weren't there in the moments of greatest need, and when you gave me permission and announced to me: "we're going to spend tonight together" I accepted your permission without illusion, without passion, like one of the so many different forms of affection that reached me with an undercurrent of tension, and I accepted this permission a little fearfully and with the mistaken insistence on wanting to hold onto something now inadequate for the purpose of filling a vacuum; but being close to you, Chachi, despite and even if it were through that strange kind of permission, was to be close to something much loved, most loved, Chachi, and what occurred, Chachita, was that I gave what was most pure and most beautiful in me, and which very quickly left me with a strong feeling of doubt, an almost shameful timidity, and I stayed like this, hardly breathing, as if searching for a corner in which to hide from my imminent exile; in Sunnyside I told myself that you had left your strange eccentricities behind in Westchester, the first of which occurred in that restaurant to which my memory gives, perhaps erroneously, the name Squire Restaurant, where I felt a serenity bordering on contentment seated there, opposite you, waiting for them to bring the lobster platter, and suddenly you said with a barely suppressed urgency, "let's go, we must go, I'm not well, I'm not feeling at all well;" the lobsters got into a box and we got into our car, and travelled the short distance to South Highland Avenue, to number 87 to be exact, the gardens made beautiful by the light of the street lamps, the anguish as we climbed, almost counting the stairs one by one; the B-25 on the black door, we entered, sat on the wide bed, you clutching a rosary, you ask me to hug you and that's what I do, tightly, and you speak of the terror that overwhelms you and you ask for protection in your hug, and I speak, trying to choose words that might occur to God, to any saint, while I too conquer my fear that you will loose control completely and with no-one to call on for help on that Sunday and the heartfelt pain, Chachita, at the very idea that you might loose your mind because you always said to me that you knew that reality was there, but that for you, this reality no longer existed; and one day while we were bathing, the same thing happened, you had to get out of the bath because you weren't feeling well, not at all well and frightened of everything, even of me, and once again the prayers and the hug that you asked me for so helplessly; in the following months, the fear remained, gripping you, until you consulted Emilio, week after week, and he began to cure you, although I don't know how, Chachita, because you never told me; and that's where my anguish stems from, my constant fear that the fragile glass separating you from insanity would weaken and I told myself that perhaps this happened to you because of your obsession with having been born out of your parents' sexual filth and you cried inconsolably because you were the product of that filth, and at other times I told myself that it was because of the acts of witchcraft your mother made you commit when you were little and, years later, my anguish was even greater when, now separated, you told me all that was the weight of your guilt for me, about me, towards me; although when I think of it, Chachi, I doubt that you loved me enough to go crazy because you felt that you didn't answer my need to share my life as a lover, because you must remember, Chachita, that if you had truly loved me, you would not have left me, years later, when they discharged me from the Blessed Virgin Mary Hospital in that neighbourhood known as Jamaica, that 21 of February, in the year 1985 in which I remember my panic, Chachi, when the day I was due to leave drew near and you said nothing about coming to fetch me and I watched the snow falling from my hospital window and felt too vulnerable to walk in it, having been so recently operated on and a lumbar disk removed, with my back full of stitches, with no-one to look after me, Chachi, and all because of your resentment towards me because I had refused to allow you to make me accept a foreign presence in my home; I listened to your voice on the telephone telling me that the day of my release you were going to a museum, I asked the doctor to let me stay in the hospital a little longer, to see if someone would come, Chachi, but they wouldn't allow it and my fear remained, intense, until Anaís offered to fetch me, which she did; that's why I have just decided, Chachi, that it's high time I got rid of the anguish of my guilt over your crises because perhaps the one who gave you that idea was Narcissa, because she never forgave me for our relationship, Chachi, that union between you and I which she viewed, when we met her, as something sacred that denied her access to you, that denied her the possibility of winning you, or that's what she told me one day, if you want to find the reasons for Chachita's crises, look for them in yourself; ours was a strange union, a strong bond always on the point of undoing itself, always ready to disappear and that's how I felt in the Agra Fort, so close to the Yamuna River, where the Shah Jehan spent his last years, after being deposed, searching with his eyes for the soul of his love which remains in the cenotaph that is kept beneath the dome of the Taj Mahal; while the guide was showing us the spaces in the walls of the Fort which before had been full of jewels, and the niches where mirrors were placed so as to create more light, I leant out of the window that the Shah Jehan must have leant out of so many times, I looked for what he would have looked for so many times, and I was startled by a profound sadness in the dusk; upon returning to Sunnyside I had the impression, though I never told you this, that a beautiful dream had been left behind, just as the gaze of my watchful eyes had remained at the window in Agra; we went up the stairs, everything in the apartment was the same: the bath, the kitchen, the rooms, everything was in its place and yet everything was different, almost alien; in the lounge, the fish tank full of dead fish: the person in whose care they had been left hadn't fed them and they floated in the tank, swollen, still covered in their reddish gold; they all saw him pass by, in a hurry, on his way to the river, and more than one person commented, there goes Peter the Long to recite one of his litanies; he reached the bridge with a nervous stealth and he settled down to listen to: "the dew of no death gnaws the harp of your ribs, spaces excavated with so much absence opened abysses in the wide rectangle; ultra-black alcohol and malachite dust are not enough to cover the death that hides itself in your eyes and which you will never be able to catch;" and with this message which he received for the first time, without knowing its origin, an electric current zigzagged up his spine and he didn't know whether his heart expanded or shrank, but it escaped from his mouth, like a bark

NERI

he only knew that they called him Neri or Nerito and that he was once three years old and that his powerful and dearly loved mama would have to die, he knew not when, he only knew that in his frequent visions he saw her strangled, her already motionless body clinging to that obstinacy that characterized her, laid out on an enormous sea shell, allowing herself to be borne off on the waves, allowing her gauze robes to be commanded by the wind; one side of the open shell bears his mother's body, the other, upright, open at right angles as if to serve as a wall; Neri or Nerito was a solitary boy who liked to spy through cracks in windows, he had already peeped through every window and had seen urinals, erect penises, some mothers' breasts spilling milk, the huge rear end of an ox, the pitch black triangle of one of his nursemaids; but none of this had captured his attention; only the tiny, left foot of that baby in its crib, waving, waving with the little kicks in the air that the baby gave, and he repeatedly returned to that window to reaffirm his promise that one day he would devour the foot of an infant not more than a few months old, so that later he could stop and examine the bloody stump, and listen to the baby's cry become a shriek, and at that moment when the baby's desperation peaked, Neri would feel remorse and sob in his convulsive manner, he would break out in a sweat, the tingling would start, the jet would stain his silk robes, and finally, total peace, Neri, because you were capable of taking pity on the bloody stump, because you were able to convulse and cry; Neri knew that all of this would come to pass and, at the age of three he savoured this knowledge with anticipation; Neri had already peeped through every window with the exception of one very ugly, peeling window; he never approached this window, mainly because he was repulsed by that particular shade of green, because he couldn't resign himself to look at the shine of the oil paint in which there were plenty of grease stains that had even seeped into the sloughs of dried paint; although the shutter was made out of planks with cracks between them, Neri told himself that the whole shutter resembled a piece of rotten, green skin; but today, at nine o'clock in the morning, while repeating to himself the bit about the putrefaction of the green skin, he also began telling himself that he could not allow time to continue passing without seeing what was behind this window and he set about preparing for the business of opening it: on his first trip to his room, he brought back a small table; on the second trip, he brought a small bench; on the third trip, he brought his chamber pot where his nursemaid made him urinate every night three and even four times; he set about arranging all of this so that the chamber pot would serve as an upside-down ciborium and without giving it any further thought, he began the task of climbing his recently constructed stairs and then, at the correct height, it was easy to undo the bolts; one tug and the shutter was no longer there and, in its place, was a square space, and in the right hand corner, lower down, Neri's head settled itself so as to observe everything, to watch, at length, that patio or waiting room painted in rotten green and the long benches for waiting, also green, unadorned, without backs; Neri did not move from his position because he knew that at any moment something, to which he was to be a witness, was going to take place, and before completing this presentiment he saw there, seated on one of the benches, a grotesquely made-up woman, the flabbiness of her skin showing the abuses of a sleepless life, the crossed legs, the skirt raised to her knees, as if to allow him to examine at his leisure what a woman's thighs are like, and his indifference to all this; the woman remained perched there, smoking, sadly showing off her make-up; and now it's my turn to speak, and I walk up to this human debris, Belkis, how can you live like this? doesn't being with so many men become unbearable? Belkis gestures with her cigarette, shrugs her shoulder blades with a resignation that leaves no room for hope; and then, for this woman I intuitively recognized as my sister, I switch off my voice and distance myself a little shamefully because I know that Neri has been present as a witness, that Neri has been aware of my voice which defines him by the power of my word; Neri has survived the vibrations made by my voice and remains there, glued to the window until the moment when the matron arrives with 15 prematurely deteriorated women, and directs them to the room next to the waiting room into which they all disappear followed by Belkis; the matron, with one gesture, orders all the men waiting in the passage to go into the same room, the last in is an American sailor in a wheel chair; Neri has watched the matron leave, has seen the door leading to the room closed and a window opened; making the most of the benches' proximity, Neri jumps down, crosses the waiting room in the direction of the opposite window, and climbs up to have a look: the men and women, naked, the women on one side, the men on another, lying down on the ground, doing callisthenics; the crippled sailor was on top of one of the women, moving in and out in her, of her, and the woman, making an effort to smile, forcing a smile; Neri moved away, none of this interested him; he used the benches to get back into his palace knowing that, most definitely, pleasure lies in compassion: to devour children, to burn men and later, to weep for them, to allow himself to be invaded by convulsive sobbing and to feel the peace of his damp robes when the men begin, with their fat, to light the roman circus the story had been started by none other than Peter the Long himself and one, two and even three people testified to this fact, but some said that it was all one of Musaraña's tales and others said that, even if it were true that Peter the Long had told this story, this did not mean that Musaraña was right in what he said: that the protagonist of the story was none other than Peter the Long himself; Musaraña stated that he had heard the story whilst hiding behind a buttress under the bridge one starry night when Peter, seated on the huge boulder in the Guaso, spoke stirringly to an invisible audience about the passage of the circus through the village of Caimanera, situated near the El Deseo Salt Pan, after which historical and relevant fact the esteemed Don Juan Ambrosio Cabral y Montes de Oca, of unknown origin, proceeded to name his new-born daughter, having her registered in the respective municipal court under the name of María del Deseo Cabral, although in reality, María del Deseo had been born in the Town of María la Grande, so named in honour of the owner of the prestigious María la Grande brothel, situated in that area known by all as `the zone'; Don Juan Ambrosio Cabral y Montes de Oca had planned to travel to Canada at some point in his life and there to adopt a little girl with blonde hair and blue eyes, just as Doctor Pavía had once done, thereby becoming the talk and envy of Guaso Town, but in view of the enormous expense this would entail, he opted instead for engendering her himself and thus María del Deseo Cabral arrived in the world, the child of an unknown mother and a father famous for having coined a new form of greeting: "Hell of a Good Day," always accompanied by the touch of the thumb of his right hand to the brim of his derby, in a show of elegance while, with his left hand, slightly raising the left tail of his dress coat; as the years passed, Don Juan Ambrosio Cabral y Montes de Oca began extending his greeting of a Hell of a Good Day more and more, shortening the interval between repetitions until it turned into a litany that increased in volume to such an extent that it deafened several citizens who, in turn, ordered him to die, which he did, obediently, climbing to the top of a mountain of salt in that same Deseo where his daughter, loyal to the Desire Salt Pan she had been named after, had, years before, provoked several sailors and lost her honour on the salt crystals and continued to loose it many more times; once on top of the white mountain, Don Juan Ambrosio Cabral y Montes de Oca, following their orders, decided to announce his death: "on these crystals, on these diamonds, with my tail coat and my hat, I hereby diminish;" and he began shrinking and shrinking until he disappeared; days later, Miss María del Deseo Cabral, member of the oldest profession, currently residing in the House of María la Grande, went to fetch, with considerable indifference, the death certificate that tersely certified that Don Juan Ambrosio Cabral y Montes de Oca had died of dematerialization and "so certified by myself that it may be officially recorded, signed by Juan Pérez, District Judge;" but all this was a game, or almost a game, because Don Juan Ambrosio Cabral y Montes de Oca continued to greet people with his Hell of a

Good Day even though his voice was now very faint, so that it bothered no-one and appeared out of unexpected places, usually out of the thumb touching the narrow brim of his derby; Peter the Long could see it all quite clearly: what had gone before, what had occurred later and what was taking place now, while perhaps suffering from ubiquity, because he who wants nothing gets everything and appears in this world with two simultaneous re-incarnations, and Don Juan Ambrosio Cabral y Montes de Oca was also, and at the same time, Tomás Reynosa; and María del Deseo Cabral was also, and at the same time, María San José Reynosa; and the Town of María la Grande was also, and at the same time, the Town of San José of the South, so named in honour of the nuns of San José Orphanage; no-one knew where Tomás Reynosa had sprung from, but he was said to have committed all kinds of atrocities, which the town half forgave him for because one day, overnight, he decided to procreate and brought into this world a baby girl of unknown mother to which the name María San José was given in honour of those saints from the Orphanage; they say that he was the son of a gypsy woman born in Cologne, known by the nickname *Agriaspenas*, that is to say Bitterpain, who had married many, many times, always searching for the best future for the son that Enobarbo had left her, until finally she decided to marry her own uncle, Don Cojo, who at the time had become the most powerful potentate in the whole region; Don Cojo adopted the boy and called him, affectionately, Reynito, his little king, but something bothered Bitterpain most profoundly: all that money and all Don Cojo's power would be wasted on two such repulsive beings as Don Cojo's son and daughter: Britico and Tavita; there was nothing for it but to call Lucumia, authority on all poisonous potions that had been discovered up till then, to take charge of sending Don Cojo on his way to the next world, which she did, with a pheasant stuffed with partridge that Don Cojo had time to praise with great happiness and appreciation but once and before taking a second bite; Bitterpain was half satisfied because, although she would have wished to be able to announce, as she usually did when a problem had been solved, that "the coffee has perked," the truth was that Britico and Tavita were still around, and presented a threat with respect to the inheritance, and something would have to be done; this time it was Reynito who took charge of solving the problem and who sent for Lucumia to dispatch Britico with one of her potions which, to vary the previous approach, she prepared in a partridge with pheasant stuffing which Britico, like his father, was able to praise just once before being reunited with Don Cojo; and for greater security, Reynito decided to marry Tavita so that his mother could say, once and for all, that the coffee had finally perked; with the passage of time, Bitterpain grew bolder and wanted to make all the decisions, and Reynito decided to do away with her too, sending her off in a sailing boat that he intended to have sunk once it reached the open sea, but the boatman, confused and unable to believe that the new potentate had given the order to kill his own mother, took her for a cruise and sang to her beneath the moon in the manner of the gondoliers of Venice and then, returned her once again to shore, safe, sound and stronger than ever; despairing at the sight of Bitterpain, Reynito urgently summoned the dwarf Centén so that, with one cut of the knife, he would commit hara kiri on Bitterpain; this, Centén set out to do while Bitterpain urinated just before going to bed as she was wont to do, standing up, between two jasmine bushes; he appeared before her with an enormous shaving knife and, throwing back his head, shouted up to her: "this is from Reynito;" and before making the cut, he heard a voice which came from above: "prick, prick here, over here, so as to eradicate all trace of the monster," and so saying, in a solemn voice, showed him the navel; upon obeying the order, Centén the dwarf watched as an enormous rat flew out of the open stomach and, in the blink of an eye, devoured a large part of his face and Centén fled, howling, and swore to himself that from that moment on, he would never again approach a breeding ground for monsters; three years after the death of Bitterpain, very early one morning, they found Tavita dead in the garden; although letters and cards of condolence poured in from all over the region, it was understood and everyone knew: this death is the work of Reynito, but no-one can accuse a potentate and they continued laughing at the things he said, applauding his talent as an actor, encouraging him to continue learning from the Philosopher who was so stoic, so good, so wise, so intelligent and when they continued with their eulogies Reynito could stand it no more and made the Philosopher commit suicide by opening his veins between the two jasmine bushes where his mother, Bitterpain, had urinated so many times; until one day, made sick by the tediousness of life, he set fire to everything and went out into the world with the circus that he had bought himself and, for the sake of art gave free shows several times a day, from three in the afternoon until eight in the evening; all of this is what they said about Tomás Reynosa, although when it comes to knowing, knowing without a shadow of a doubt, all that was really known was that he had appeared in the Town of San José of the South where one day it would occur to him to beget María San José Reynosa, of unknown mother, who followed the straight and narrow path and ended up becoming a nun in the San José

Orphanage and a model of virtue; Reynosa's circus, to which less and less people went because it was becoming somewhat sadistic and obscene, was not far from the Orphanage; Tomás Reynosa was given to relating that an Indian with a very light, although not white skin, underwent an operation in the San Agustín hospital and the Indian got such a fright thinking that they had amputated his penis that, when he came around from the anaesthetic, there in the recovery room and in front of everyone, he grabbed his naked penis and with desperate joy said: "it's here, it's still here, it's whole," and with this story about the recovery room that Tomás Reynosa liked to refer to in the eight o'clock show, while standing on the tail of an alligator and wearing a toga, he grabbed his penis and moved it until strange things began occurring which made children and old ladies cry from terror until one day, a group of soldiers, respectful of the young and the elderly, gave him a Coup d'Etat in the middle of the circus, in the middle of the eight o'clock show, and he decided to commit suicide by allowing himself to be swallowed by the alligator, but they were not able to verify whether or not it was a final death because, a few days later, an old lady arrived home in tears saying that someone had told her an indecent tale about an Indian in a recovery room and then, and then, everyone knew; what no-one knew was that the only one who was aware of these multiple re-incarnations was Don Juan Ambrosio Cabral y Montes de Oca who decided to ignore Tomás Reynosa and María del Deseo, and was left with the distress caused by not being able to communicate with his twin soul, the soul of María San José, and who, as a sign of mourning, walked kilometres until, arriving at the Guaso, he removed his derby, hid his head in his hands, holding his forehead, and began to cry while listening to the water splash; hardly had a few weeks

passed when the trial of Musaraña took place, a trial by street-
court in which he was asked to present conclusive evidence
concerning the identity of Peter the Long, there present, and
his relationship with the multiple re-incarnations, and if not
able to do so, he was to be condemned to death by announcing
his own death; Musaraña began by stating that conclusive
evidence did exist: Peter the Long had said that Don Juan
Ambrosio Cabral and Montes de Oca, like Tomás Reynosa,
was of unknown origin, but he knew as much about their
lives as he did about his own; and furthermore, Juan Ambrosio
had been to cry in the Guaso just like Peter the Long did so
many times; confronted with the threatening looks of the
people around him, Musaraña recanted, he told them that he
didn't have the imagination to invent death formulas and he
then repeated, under oath, the exact words that Peter the Long
had pronounced that starry night: "I'm beginning to confuse
old ladies and tomatoes, creepers and umbrellas; as human
beings we smell fear, like dogs; but today I want to concentrate
on breathing time; I can't think clearly if I don't take two
Anacins: it's as if my head contained a few embryonic pieces
of pain; I'm a baby goat, unperemptory and sunshade; I'm the
little cockatoo with chrysanthemum colours; those midgets
are going to mount three parrots; Torcuata Remembrada,
Eusebia Limón, the sex of little Moorish girls is tightly closed;
I am Mondonguito Tribilín; I don't know whether to pull out
your tooth, pull off your spectacles or pull three hairs from
where it hurts most; like a nanny goat's nipples, mules and
burning stones; pour sauter du coq à l'âne, to jump from the
cock to the ass or, to change topics, je m'en fous dans une
incongruité, I'm fucked in an incongruence, tous les jours,
every day, comme dans un coup de foudre, like bolt of
lightening; from their hiding place in the cupboards, they

flew out and invaded the catacombs; and after all, to remember that cockroach that for so many years lived, trapped in the hollow of the armpit, and to face up to the discovery that ants from South Africa are crazy about egg yolk;" and I will always remember, Chachita, when you were asleep and I asked you silly things and you answered me so seriously and with such effort, without waking up: where do you think you are, in a cornfield? no, I'm with the trees, but I threw them away; and why did you throw them away? because they can't talk; and what do you want them to say? they must say "mommy;" and who filled the room with chickens? the old man from the corner; what old man? the old man with the cane; and in this way, Chachita, I kept myself horribly amused and I forgot about those monstrous things that were in me, because there's no worse crime than sadness because there's no greater monster than the absence of happiness, and just think, Chachi, that since I was a little girl, at the time when I peered through the cracks in the houses to search for adventures, I knew that sadness existed and I asked myself day after day, I promise you, Chachi, day after day, what would it be like to be in someone else's skin, what would it be like to inhabit a body and a mind that were free of sadness; and whenever I felt clumsy before you, I was invaded by that insecurity and that profound, black silence that you feared, as I feared it too because I wasn't able to break free of it; until one day when you returned exhausted from Manhattan and I was in one of my silences, you asked me, almost crying, not to reject you and then I understood that the hurt I was causing you, and causing myself, had to end, and I tried and thought I had changed although I don't know if you noticed, Chachita, because you never said so, but that I thought I had changed, yes I did believe it, and this, Chachi, I swear to you; and finally and to his relief, Musaraña listened to the decision taken by the street-court sitting in judgement on him: "in view of the fact that you have been forthcoming in showing the everyday thought, word and work of Peter the Long, you are free to go, Mr Musaraña, to wander the streets, aimlessly"

OLLANTAITAMBO

the *amauta*, the Inca elder, tells my story which never passed
to the quipu, those knotted cords which store our history;
his unknotted mouth lets loose an echo of words that escape
from the *quipucamayu*, the keeper of the quipus, because
they must remain in the air in order to retain transparency,
like the molecules of my body which weightlessly beat the
Andean air; when I am outside of the Inca elder's voice, I
momentarily draw near to the tired stone, seated in its
enormity, still crying at the impossibility of ascending to the
Cuzco to be part of its massive structure; I reach the peak of
the Sierra that they used to call Uillacanuta, and suspended
in mid air I explore its pyramidal parameter; I left my slavery,
I buried forever the job of servant, of *yanacuna*; my room is
the open space and my paths the currents of the Apurímac
and the Urubamba; but the *amauta* says that I am a legend,
and surrounded by his audience I am trapped by his voice,
he confines me to the sound he makes: "each night, for many
centuries, in the Ollantaitambo Valley, wrapped in her blanket,
seated on the humid ground, the Indian woman awaited the
arrival of her lover, just as Mother Night had promised her;
she carried in her arms a moon child, who searches amongst

the stars for the eyes of his father, Swift Fawn, as he had learnt to do during the eternity of his ten months, finding nourishment in the litany trapped faintly in the throat of the beautiful Indian: *child, my child, may your eyes retain the stars that will guide with their light the one whose absence we mourn today;* but the Indians from the villages speak of having seen the poncho and sandals on the transparent body until it blended with the mist, the diluted silhouette of Swift Fawn that approached them, and when they speak to him, their voices make him disappear, their looks cause him to run away to find his woman that the night had stolen from him; and they tell of an occasion when once, at dusk, they saw his figure in the shadows, following the diluted smudge of a light that went further into the Ollantaitambo Valley; there, seated, protected by her blanket, the woman and the child; the Indian, still at a distance, allowed his lament to be heard: *let my echo touch you, beautiful woman, halt this journey that becomes fatigue, you carry in your arms the kiss of our lips and I carry in my skin the juice of your body;* but they say that when the beautiful woman sensed his voice and wanted to find him, her eyes could only make out the great emptiness of the night;" and now the *amauta* releases me from his voice and I can be mist on the snowy peaks, morning dew in the valleys, swift coolness in currents of the Apurímac and the Urubamba; eternal nostalgia in the closed night of the Ollantaitambo his name was Juan Lucumí, a free African in the year 1784, 34 years old and husband to Gonzala Lucumí, slave from the Felicia Sugar Mill; the year was already quite advanced and, since June, he had given five hundred pesos to the Santa María del Rosario *síndico,* a functionary who represents the slaves in legal matters, to finish paying for the above mentioned Gonzala, a Black woman who, for many years, had participated in this system of *coartación* by which a slave could buy his or her freedom; she had given an initial amount towards buying herself back and had been able to continue paying because she enjoyed the privileges of a coartada and it was not possible to raise the price originally placed on her person and moreover, if another master employed her, he gave her a small wage which she religiously saved in order to break the chains, as she used to say; but time passed and Gonzala Lucumí still had not received the letter granting her freedom, stuck in the slave quarters, in the big, rectangular house, sealed so hermetically at night to prevent escape, and when it was full moon, her avid eyes searched the chipped walls looking for crevices through which to see the light of Mother Moon that, in some corner of the world, would be shining on Juan Lucumí; she knew that the moon would carry her rays as far as Santa María del Rosario where Juan was, stationed in front of that door, reminding the *síndico,* I, five hundred pesos, freedom, the *coartada,* Gonzala Lucumí; but silence always met his protest that was becoming hoarse and went snaking through the air to the ears of the Governor who quite easily gave himself to the task of ignoring it; furthermore, just as the former masters had the right to give orders to the freed slaves, Juan Lucumí was prohibited from approaching the Felicia Sugar Mill until the case had been decided and Juan Lucumí did not know that his son had been born and that, thanks to the compassion of the mulatto, Calisto, who was the quarter's custodian, Gonzala was able to take her son outside one night and offer him to Mother Moon; years passed and Juan Lucumí continued appealing to Societies of the Coloured Race: the Society for Equality, the Society of the Light, the Society of Friendship, The Daughters of Progress; he appealed to newspapers and magazines to petition for his rights, and that cry of his with which he called his wife appeared in *Minerva,* the fortnightly magazine dedicated to the Coloured Woman; *The Torch* from Trinidad; *The Fraternity; Aurora of the Yumurí;* he also appealed to the Congo Council, to the *Arriero* Council of the Ganga Mongoba Nation and other groups that, under the name of Councils, preserved nuclei of culture and religion from the distant regions of Africa; he invoked the Orishas, made offerings of all that he thought would please them, but one night of *batá,* the fierce rhythm of the drums echoed in his chest and the moon, risen over the yard of the Sugar Mill, watched him cry because a few hours before he had read of the case of María Josefa de la Luz Hernández and the legal proceedings which were instituted in 1802 in order to prevent her marriage because it was known that, although she had a white skin, she was descended from the mulatto Rosenda Neyra, the rich, so very rich owner of the Our Lady of the Candlemas Sugar Mill, and the family of her white fiance stopped the wedding because a mulatto loaded with gold is still a mulatto and María Josefa de la Luz would remain a mulatto and colour did not combine well with *criollos,* whites descended from Spanish colonizers, oh no, not that, and thus the legal proceedings against her; yes, Juan Lucumí, convince yourself that the official powers that stood in the way of María Josefa de la Luz, stand in your way too and one fine day they will tell you that your petition has expired and that you must start again because the *síndico* does not remember having received 500 pesos; convince yourself, that years may pass with you working as a boiler at one of the sugar mills or in some tobacco factory in the position of twister, selector, stem remover, making cigar bands, panatellas or whatever they would tell him to do with the different leaves of tobacco: the eighteenth of Vuelta Abajo or the sixteenth or seventeenth or the eighth of Remedios and to jump from H. Upmann to Gener and from Gener to Partagás and from Partagás to Trinidad and Brothers and to work in tobacco sweat shops with that strange crew which includes Chinamen, Yucatecans, black slaves and freed slaves and to hurry, to always hurry so as to fill the quota of three hundred huge cigars each day, without being consoled even by the voice of the reader during his hour of reading in the morning, in his hour of reading in the afternoon, until one day he decided to tear up the account book where his perennial debt to the company was written and escaped in an enormous pumpkin full of lit candles, navigating against the current in the Cauto River, towards the East, wrapped in a blue cloak in honour of the two water orishas: Oshún and Yemayá; now in the Oriente Province, he headed for the mountains and climbed the 6,560 feet to the top of Turquino to make himself mist, to condense into clouds and to fall as a fine rain on the enormous rock in the Guaso; it was an 8th of September and Peter the Long was seated on a stool, leaning against the wall, on a porch that faced onto the street, watching the processions go by and the celebrations organised to honour Our Lady of Mercy of Cobre just as they were celebrating the festival of Our Lady of Regla in Havana that same day; little by little the two benches in the porch began to fill up with other spectators who had brought with them, to liven up the period of waiting, several *buchitos* of coffee, bought in the Petit Miami, served in minuscule paper cups, so tiny that they looked like thimbles; the conversation inevitably turned to the two Virgins, water orishas, and shortly thereafter, to the legend of Juan Lucumí, navigating the Cauto in the pumpkin of the orisha Oshún, Virgen of the Mercy of Cobre, patron of our people; wrapped in a blue cloak, the colour of Yemayá, orisha of Havana Bay, Virgin of Regla; Peter the Long's grip tightened on his *buchito* when he heard the question, and you, Peter, what do you think of the legend of Juan Lucumí, Navigator of the Cauto? Peter the Long gritted his teeth crushing the tiny paper cup before removing it from his mouth and began shouting for Gonzala Lucumí, a name unknown to the people there present and to make anguished promises, also shouting, in which he guaranteed having handed in 500 pesos, promises that no-one understood but which they did not try to understand on that day when what was important were the processions and celebrations; Peter the Long felt, as he had many times before, an unstoppable desire to disappear and he rushed off, towards the river; on the huge rock, with his arms extended, he projected his solitary voice: "numeric weight, disguised hope, bottled destiny, twisted table, hirsute state, surprised virgo, spiral lip, incipient marsupial, pouch bag, intermittent lunar calendar, vegetable rebel, reptile vision, distressed intention, remunerated lay sister, jumping sound, escape chain, wheat field memory, submerged labyrinth, biting space, distributed vicissitudes, calming redeemer, sacred epistle, verbal incision, escape chain, escape, escape;" he had spent hours there, standing on the rock, with his arms forming a cross, before realising that he existed and was there, as alive as always; nobody saw him during the eight day celebrations and, on the ninth day, when the town was beginning to worry, a farm worker who had come to town to do some shopping, dressed in a white *guayabera* and a Cuban Liborio hat, was certain that he had seen him pass by his hut heading towards the mountains; and that was what we did tirelessly in Mexico, Chachi, climb up and down pyramids in that year of 1976, when the aeroplane landed us in the city of the Fiesta Palace, of the Palace of Chapultepec, the Church of San Francisco, the Zócalo, Las Lomas, where Beto, the guide, assured us we would find the houses of Dolores del Río, Frank Sinatra and Marlon Brando; the next day, with Enrique, in Tula, Tollán, we passed the wall of serpents, carved skulls, the eagle with the heart in its mouth; the Atlantes guarding the land of the Toltecs, we peered at the mystery of Chac-Mool, at the changing features of Quetzalcoatl; do you remember, Chachi, the Monastery of Saint Francisco Javier in Tepotzotlán? from the balcony of that restaurant on the second floor we saw the courtyard of the creepers and the large earthenware jars; we got stuck into our lunch of chicken consomé with avocado, Tampico steak with beans sprinkled with cheese, a taco, creme caramel and coffee with cinnamon; in Xochimilco, the hail beating on the launch dressed in flowers and one little Indian in her canoe going from launch to launch looking for shelter; now in Room 1210 of the Fiesta Palace, I follow Enrique's advice: take some aspirins and give yourself a hot shower to take the chill from your bones after so much hail; now in the wide bed, we made love without your having announced to me what I now recognize for what it was back then, Chachi, the sacrifice of your permission, and I went to that moment with the vague idea of sealing something without even knowing what it was, and coming out of the moment, I put a smile on my face that deep down was full of questions and empty space, because I knew that we had been unable to stop your drawing further away which was born, perhaps, out of the bulge of my belly, my untidy clothes, the chaotic disorder that I sow in our apartment, from my unbearable silences, from the rejection that you feel towards your mother and that you began extending towards me; on the television they were saying that Princess Anne had fallen from her horse and they announced the results of the Olympic games; Oaxaca, Mitla, Mount Albán, Villahermosa, Palenque, la Venta, Mérida, Kabah, Chichén Itzá, Uxmal, the paradise of Cozumel, Room 410 in the Hotel Presidente, the fine sand, the vastness of the sea and a sound of palms and waves; at dinner time we went down to the hotel's only restaurant which seemed to have come out of one of those movies from the 40's in which a luxurious ambience was the norm and where the crowd moved without a care, sans souci, or only concerned with its intrigues of passion, alien to poverty, to social questions; the walls of the restaurant were all of glass with a view towards the beach, towards the vastness of sand and sea; the dining room was lit with huge candles, repeated in different colours, grouped near the piano, on a high platform from where they gave off their mysterious air, as if they were a gathering of nuns giving off a light almost alive with waves of prayer sealed in their silence; the trio, accompanying themselves with guitars, plays romantic songs until making way for a piano solo like those you see in films showing some crooning corner of New Orleans; before me stands the maître d'hôtel, small, thin, with olive coloured skin, who could easily play the part of the oriental bad guy in any of Sydney Greenstreet's movies, an expert in the use of the mysterious dagger, stabbed into a back covered by a suit of white drill; he gestures that he is ready to take our order, pencil and pad in hand, lips sealed in a straight grimace, horizontal, rigid; every day, an enormous breakfast in the hotel and afterwards, to paradise, to the blue-green waters, transparent so that we can see the stones on the bottom; on the third day, an excursion to Robinson Crusoe; we board the enormous motor boat, several hours of cruising and half way there, three men equipped with spears throw themselves into the sea and the fat man who pilots the boat explains, they're going to bring us our lunch; the boat waits, motor running, while the men bring all kinds of fish, a huge quantity of enormous, reddish conches; they prepare and clean everything there in that same boat; when we arrive at Robinson Crusoe, we swim in the sea while a man cooks everything they brought from the sea in huge pots over charcoal grills, making *enchilado de mariscos,* a type of spicy seafood stew like the one they make in Cuba; after swimming, hunger accompanies us to the rustic tables under a roof of palm leaves; on the fourth day we take a taxi to the centre of Cozumel after I refuse your suggestion that we make the trip on hired motorbikes; we walk the streets, the town moves slowly as if it were crawling; a series of kiosks, in one of them a man shows huge jaws of sharks; I speak to him expecting him to tell in horror of the dangers of his job, but he, as if it were nothing, listen, it happens that I'm going out to catch sharks tomorrow, would you like to come? that's very kind of you but, no, thank you, and we continue walking and decide to hire a vehicle constructed of two parallel bicycles attached to a kind of large wooden box; a sense of freedom, we capriciously choose any direction, and stop to have dinner in one of those restaurants, the one that seems most acceptable to us; once inside, the hopelessness of trying to chase off the flies that land on the tablecloth, the serviettes, the cutlery; we order a dish that we don't recognise which turns out to be a crumbed ham steak, greasy, that we decided to eat out of hunger, until I see an expression of disgust on your face as you hear something crunching under your knife, a fried cockroach hidden in the breadcrumbs of the ham; the waiter makes a quick backwards movement, a gesture of disgust, apologizes, I won't charge you for this dish; and I felt guilty for years, for many years, Chachi, for not being able to prevent it from happening, for not having suggested, let's eat in the hotel restaurant where something like that would not have happened, and even today that I don't know where you are or if you are anywhere, I can hardly forgive myself for that, I swear to you, Chachi, I swear; we left without eating, without seeing the aquarium; from our room in the hotel we ordered a turkey sandwich that arrived badly made with stale bread; decidedly, I haven't been right in anything and I'm a little embarrassed in front of you; the next day, at two pm, Aeronaves de Mexico's flight 251 takes me away from Cozumel with the near certainty that you have stayed behind, in the transparent water, this 5th of August

HUNG-WU

what does it matter if they call me Hung-Wu, I will always
be the humble Chu Yuang-Chang; in my emperor's silks I
walk the country paths, I return at my beggar's pace, I am a
buddhist monk, I am the humble peasant at the hour of tea,
seated amongst cushions in my emperor's hall, at the hour
when I grow weary of these heads bowing to me, the hour at
which I allow Hui-ti to raise his little head behind the main
folding screen, to spy on me coquettishly, to delight in playing
with me without drawing near, without speaking, allowing
his young head to escape from my view when I show surprise
as if I had just noticed him for the first time; Hui-ti would
continue playing forever, Hui-ti, the inexhaustible; but now
a reluctance to continue playing climbs my beard that rests at
the level of my stomach; the movement of Hui-ti as he moves
closer to sit before me makes me happy; Hui-ti I know how
much you would like to hear from my lips the fabulous stories
that grandfathers tell to children like you; but it is my time to
be quiet, to communicate to you without words my vision of
the Universe; discern my thought at this time of meditation:
one day, Hui-ti, you will follow the path of this dynasty of light
that I founded in Nanking; one day, Hui-ti, you will be amazed

that you shared a small cup of tea with this old man who in your eyes is the humble Chu Yuan-Chang and to others, the T'ai-tgu of the temple, the Hung-Wu of our dynasty; with you, now, I am that old man who asks himself in what have I failed, why have I failed; I have spread the words of Confucius: brotherhood, respect for my elders, for my ancestors, peace, the instruction of children; and you already know, I always practised rigorous abstinence; but I am plagued by suspicion in moments that should be beatific, I believe I hear a veiled offense against my person and I unleash my steal fist and I order a brutal punishment; and now, Hui-ti, my son, do not fear the apparent rigidity of my body, I am astral planing, goodbye, Hui-ti, and now I enter space crossing centuries, six centuries, and I do not get to see the name, Chaff, Chaff; I am seated behind a desk, inside the skin of a woman; lines of prisoners are approaching, and I ask, what was your crime, which prison did you come from, what is your religion, and already the day wears on and the interrogations continue until, seated before me, I see the man with the jet black skin, with a malevolent gleam in his eyes; with the gleam that bounces quickly off the silver caps that he wears on his teeth; his presence terrifies me, his malevolent laugh and the voice which defines him: I am a *palero,* a man who practises witchcraft using wood from the trees, my chest is crisscrossed with knife cuts and my work is carried out in the land of the dead, when I rip them from their tombs and make a pact with the devil; in a strange handwriting I record the *palero's* story while I make an effort to get myself out of this skin, to return; by an act of willpower, I project myself, I am now in the cosmos, in space, crossing the akashic records, the ones I am not supposed to see yet; everything is fine, everything will be fine when I return to the Nanking palace and the gleam from the silver caps no longer burns my pupils;

now I can see the outline of those old houses, the imperial hall, I slowly return to my old skin; sensation returns to my hands as I feel the small fingers of Hui-ti: "Grandfather, Grandfather Chu Yuan-Chang, is that gleam in your eyes bad?" "no, Hui-ti, it is the shine from the tea, it is the shine which has jumped out of the little tea cup"

Peter the Long thought about it for a bit and made a decision and did what he had to do; he headed for the park and climbed the wooden platform especially erected for that purpose; he went up to the microphone and let loose a voice that sounded like a lament: "I am not here to inform, I am here to say that the Emperors, the Sons of Heaven, lasted hundreds of years and I'm not going to confirm that I was one of them but I am saying and affirming that I was never like the Shang, who demanded that, upon their deaths, men and horses be killed to serve them in the Hereafter, and I also say and affirm that I was with many of them like a shadow and I advised them and I spoke to them without their understanding my transparency because I never bothered to explain to them that I was one more of those spirits in which they believed and, as such, I was able to be present in all ages and spaces at once, and with my bodiless voice I warned the last Manchu, Hsüan-T'ung, in that same year of 1909, you who are only three, you understand nothing, P'u-yi, they take your throne from you and I see it, and you will remain in this Forbidden City, prisoner in a golden cage, but come what may, you will continue to think it, that our race is the most advanced, our nation, the centre of the Universe, and that we are in every way, superior to those barbaric westerners, but someday you will know, P'u-yi, that

Sun Yat-Sen, with his revolution, will annihilate the Manchu and he will remain in the South, leaving us in the North to these War Lords, and everything, and all this so that Sun Yat-Sen just goes and dies in 1925 with the result that Chiang-Kai-Shek's presence would be felt in the fight against the Japanese and the Communists, introducing his Republic which will last till 1949 when everything will disappear beneath the title of Popular; and now I say it and I repeat it, that one Liu-Pang started the Han dynasty without belonging to the aristocracy and when he was born, long before our own era, they told us that he had been conceived when his mother, in a state of ecstasy, surrendered herself to a deity, and who could prove otherwise, but we did see, this we all saw, a dragon prowling around in space, above the bed which witnessed his birth; and here is what I never did: take the life of a woman who was unfaithful to me or of a disobedient child; and here is what I did indeed do: even despite myself because it is not in my nature, I bound my life to those of various wives and concubines; I had offspring just as they advised me, so as not to become a starving phantom after my death, with no one to give me a plate of food, although I must confess that hunger has followed me right to this day, in this land, because there are deep particles in my being that are not satisfied with bowls of rice, and quite despite myself, I follow this destiny that seems to consist of discovering everything that will not be given to me; that of knowing that everything is there and that it exists, but not within my reach nor for me, although I don't recall having done wrong, because each time I died, those relatives that remained alive tied my body tightly to the bed until they were sure that my spirit had detached itself, because it was known amongst us, and well known too, that otherwise, the dead body with its spirit hidden inside it would be transformed into a

zombie capable of committing evil deeds; and each time a child
was born to me, we wrapped the new born babe in an old pair
of his father's - my - trousers, to convey the knowledge of my
many years of experience to the child, and whenever it was a
male child, we would go into town to buy fresh eggs and red
paint and we celebrated his birth by offering eggs that had
been dyed red to friends who came to meet him, and whenever
it was necessary, we covered the baby's face so that the spirits,
envious of our happiness, would not hurt him in any way, and
now I, as General and Absolute President of the League Against
Evil and Other Things, declare that I have called a meeting;"
but at that moment Peter the Long disappeared along with the
platform and the microphone, and days later people commented
that Peter the Long and his audience were there, in front of
everyone's eyes, during the speech's introduction and conclusion,
and that in the opening statements he began to speak of what
appeared to be his past as a Chinaman, mentioning in passing
emperors and political figures among which we all recognised
one Chiang-Kai-Shek that we had seen appear in the magazine
Bohemia; and that was all that Musaraña needed to hear in
order to decide to present his conclusive case against Peter the
Long; he sat down in a park bench, near the hero's statue and
began to write down, in pencil, on some crumpled and filthy
pieces of paper that he had picked up in the street: I here declare
and confirm that Peter the Long disappeared from this park in
the middle of a speech and continued speaking in mid air
where he was joined by some of those he selected from amongst
his audience, with whom he crossed the sky in triangular
formation, with Peter at the head, as apex, followed by a row
with two of the chosen, followed by a row of three of the
chosen, followed by a row of four of the chosen, followed by a
row of five of those chosen which formed the base of the

triangle; during the flight he transmitted to his fourteen followers, without speaking, some knowledge of some of the dynasties, and about the last dynasty on which he dwelt at length, and the custom that those from the North had of eating garlic wrapped in bread and the Chinese addiction to opium, and clearly, very clearly stated without words: "I was all of that and I am multiple; I am the little girl with plaits, at six, the lonely Guaso girl who spies on the Chinamen who own the restaurant in Caimanera, while they smoke opium and I am also one of the opium smokers who is being watched by her in this era in which we have all awaited, for three years, the arrival of *Gone with the Wind* at the Faust Cinema, in this era in which we have continued to laugh our heads off with Catita, the Argentinean Gallega, and in a slightly more forced manner with Luis Sandrini, in this era in which we cry convulsively and quietly with Libertad Lamarque; and to you, my fourteen chosen, I can tell this to you because you will understand me: that minutes and inches, years and kilometres, advance, regress, disperse, embrace, intertwine;" the air became warm with the friction generated by the speed of the fifteen flying arrows, Peter as apex, and at the base of the triangle, five of the Guaso citizens chosen by him; the thirty eyes passed by towns, cities, rivers, vast mountains, expanses of sea, but they did not concentrate on perceiving anything, focused always on their telepathic guide that they now secretly called the True Son of the Guaso, because of a legend that became unstoppable: he had been born there, beneath the waters, of the waters, by the waters and in them, at the moment when he was pushed from a strange portrait that cried, and this true Guaso citizen should be followed even to the ends of the earth; a few lightening flashes lit the point of arrival just like the lights that illuminate runways; the voice of the True One made the clouds shake with its thunder: "we have arrived," he said, and when his voice disappeared, the fourteen found themselves seated before a building decorated, or so they believed, with Bengal lights, until they realised that these lights, intensely yellow and orange in colour, did not move vertiginously as Bengal lights move and, to be precise, we should say that these lights were motionless although they seemed to lick at parts of the building in order to remove it from the darkness; they stayed still, in a state of ecstasy before this visual gift until the light of day brought with it a transparency in which they could make out palms, flowers, benches, iron railings: this was, definitely, a park; they slowly became aware and got to know that they had arrived in a country whose president had fallen ill and that another was in power, perhaps substituting for him permanently; they toured the city as you would tour a sunrise or Spring; they went to the Indian Market, to Indian areas, to the famous Chatsworth temple, they walked down the wide streets, they reached the avenue of King George the Fifth and wandered amongst the University's strange architecture through which they made out, running, between the trees, several Vervet monkeys; they studied the harbour so scarcely populated with ships; they went to The Valley of a Thousand Hills to see the round Zulu houses; they admired everything and enjoyed themselves immensely at each step; they also knew that between the sun, the palms and the paradisiacal beauty, there were outbreaks of Satanism, or so the newspapers said: that a sect of Satanists, mere school children, had been discovered; the same story was told by Tina, the Indian woman who sold fruit from her truck, that she had walked into a house by mistake and seen a room with the walls painted black on which were hung the heads of pigs and cats; that was what Tina said and she asserted it very clearly, in the street of Willowvale, on the corner of Manning and she confirmed as clear as clear can be that the satanic room was in Umbilo Road and that a neighbour who lived right next door to the members of the sect had told her, in secret, that her neighbours spent their time killing cats to drink their blood and to this was added the testimony of the Christian missionary, coloured, originally from Paarl East in the Cape Province, and resident of the city of Durban in a house located on the corner of Evans Street and Sir Liege, which she shares with another female missionary, also Christian, but white; the coloured missionary told the story and said that she spent her time visiting hospitals to convince doctors and nurses to treat their patients with Christian love so that each patient would be cured, not only in body, but also in soul which is sprinkled in the blood and flows through the veins, and also the spirit which is a large emptiness which must be filled with God; and she repeated the bit about the great emptiness while giving small smacks to her stomach as if to show that here is where the emptiness is, and she was left ecstatic and happy with the explanation which she had given about the difference between the soul and the spirit, and the demonstration and final proof of the emptiness in the stomach; straight away and, moreover, immediately, she made reference to a satanic sect about which she had heard, located in one of the city's hospitals and to which a majority of the hospital's nurses and doctors belonged, she also said she had been informed about it by none other than the very Head Nurse of that hospital and that also, in Cape Town, there is a group of satanists who meet on Table Mountain and who send out from there a beam of malevolent energy to sink the country, but these malevolent forces are counterbalanced by the energy from the prayers of a Christian group which meets where the Cecil John Rhodes Monument is and from where they send out powerful prayers that protect the country; but despite these malevolent outbreaks that are presented as the bad weed that we must exterminate in all countries of the world, this city of Durban has been classified by all of us, the True One and the fourteen chosen, as a beautiful city and beyond that, far beyond that: as the most beautiful city that the eyes of Guaso citizens had seen since the beginning of the world and of all worlds, until this interesting and conflict-riddled year that we call 1989; the return journey was so quick that it flashed unnoticed by the fourteen followers of the True One in the flying triangle and they found themselves, suddenly and just like that, seated in that park in Guaso Town listening to the last words of Peter the Long that left the microphone to penetrate each ear as if they were long, sharp nails: "and that's all from me and from the multiplicity of my being -which particularly today- I would like to call our being;" Musaraña had written a detailed document on his filthy and sometimes crinkled papers which he had picked up in the streets, an inventoried information sheet headed by the somewhat extensive title of: "The case of those that deceive the people saying that they are at a meeting in the park and who, however, travel through the clouds in triangular formation, and who number fifteen counting the head or guide whom they call the True One, and who reach another country in a year much further ahead in time than this in which we still have not received *Gone with the Wind* but which must be about to arrive because we have already been waiting for it for three years; and this triangle which I call phenomenal, unprecedented and also unacceptable, had the audacity to leap ahead and to live in the year 1989 and spend a few days in a foreign land as if they were on a tour organised by a travel agent and to return in time, before the sixty minutes that the meeting would have lasted because the town luxury which is the rented microphone had to be returned; and we citizens of the Guaso demand an explanation and account of the inadmissible activities from the so called True One who, on a lesser note, arrived at the Guaso with the name of Peter Matei;" and although the title seemed a little long to him, Musaraña squinted his eyes and pulled repeated and rapid faces to express some of his boundless happiness: definitively, he was most satisfied with this document that he had composed and which he secretly called the Prosecution Index of all Worthy Public Prosecutors; in an outburst of satisfaction he pointed to the document that he carried, trapped under his arm as if it were a ministerial folder or an attache case, and he said to someone who was smoking near the statue of Periquito Pérez and whom he had recognized as one of the fourteen chosen: "listen, just so that you know, I have here the case of the Flying Triangle, so prepare yourself because you are also involved;" the aforesaid smoker, who was nothing more and nothing less than a second cousin to Chicho Bota, winked at him and laughed in his face while saying to him: "leave it alone, Musa, you're getting old and you forget things, but any tribunal in which you present that piece of scrap that you are carrying there, is going to ask you where you got your information from and you are going to have to tell them that you know all this because you were one of those in the Flying Triangle, in fact, you were at my side in the right hand point of the Triangle, and in one of those moments when we were flying high and we passed over one of those very big oceans, I looked at you and the kinky curls in your hair had been straightened with the speed of our flight and that made me laugh and I thought: if Musa's curls keep straightening, he's going to come out of this with hair like a white man;" Musaraña stood, studying Chicho Bota's second cousin with some confusion, and in the midst of that confusion he seemed to recall crossing, with violent speed, a current of air and noticed, upon touching his head, that his hair, still tangled and dirty, seemed somehow docile and that was enough for him to send Chicho Bota's second cousin a farewell glance before moving off towards the river in the hopes of meeting up with Peter the Long to offer him a protocol apology, and he liked that bit about protocol, and he imagined himself saying: listen, Peter, forgive me, because this time, friend, I have indeed failed you from beginning to end and back again because after all, what you wanted was that we see what is beautiful in life and also the evil weed that we must pull out and you wanted to show us also that the four little things we see with our five senses, the only ones we believe we have, is not everything that exists in the world and in these worlds; and I swear this to you, Peter, I swear it, that if anyone comes to speak to me about the limits of our senses and comes with that story about us only living once, I am going to get as mad as a snake, and I mean spitting mad, and I am going to tell anyone who dares, listen, friend, what story is this, what false story is this; but Peter the Long was nowhere to be seen in the surrounding area and Musaraña decided to head into the *sao* that was nothing more than an abandoned plot, so overgrown and full of garbage that it looked like a dump; and there, squatting, he evacuated his intestines; then, in the river, he shouted out loud for Peter, but received absolutely no reply; he then decided to drop his trousers to give his bottom a good wash with that incessantly flowing water; a little later, he fell asleep beneath a tree in the immense night, refreshed; and I tell you, Chachita, that we did the right thing in going to Unity Village because that was a journey which I believed would lead to freedom, towards the light; we left Ossining in the yellow Pacer that was almost round and full of windows, Fatty, you called it, one Monday the 18th of July at

7:35 a.m. in the year 1977 when the Pacer was 8,555 miles old; the next day we arrived at Olentangy at 4:30 in the afternoon; we paid the entrance fee at the booth and started to descend into the humid depths of the caves, just the two of us, without other tourists, without any guides; tortured paths that continued descending, fear, a need to urinate, trousers down, freeing the body to release its stream, the two streams, yours and mine, Chachi, that made us laugh resoundingly in the echo of the caves; on the Wednesday we stopped at the Ohio Historical Center with its mastodon from the Ice Age, displays on the history of Ohio and a time capsule in which we wrote a message that will be read decades into the future when you and I will already be in other dimensions; on the way back from Unity Village we went to Hannibal to look for a trace of Mark Twain; we stayed in Hull, in a whitewashed, wooden motel in which you suffered a crying fit over the dead tortoise, for the little, dead tortoise whose death you remembered from time to time because your mother had forced you to cut its head off in one of her rituals; I felt a vague sadness when it came time to leave; driving along the roads had given me a near freedom; almost from the beginning I had been overtaken by the feeling that the true goal was the journey itself: to continue travelling ceaselessly, on an infinite journey, although I never said anything to you, perhaps because I did not know myself until now; we arrived at Ossining that evening, almost after dark

WE COULD CALL IT FLIGHT 202

the bar was dark, smoky, the darkness beat at the colours of
the Tiffany lamps which set off a bombardment of colours
red-ruby, yellow-yellow, green-emerald; one of the stools, tall,
much taller than my legs, propped me there, seated at the bar,
in front of the Grand Manier with its orange colour and taste
of oranges and the passion of alcohol and almost protective
distance in this year which could be 1920 but which was more
likely 1985, when I was woman and I fed myself on carrots
and vegetables that sprouted stealthily from the pavements,
from the windows of some subway, from the railway tracks,
from the prow of some ship; I would go out, till an indeterminate
hour, to comb for the presence of any leaf, a stalk of celery,
which I detest, something nourishing, and then the painful
process began, to inject this into my fingernails, volatilizing it
first, invisibilizing it, making the carbohydrates invisible, the
chlorophyll, some protein lost in the small mound of vegetable,
nourishment, one could say, vaporised, trained, watching it
travel the length of the nail until it is lost from sight beneath
the cuticles and to feel it move then, eventually, to the flow of
some current of blood; all this always took place in absolute
secrecy in the kitchen in Sunnyside, in the top-floor apartment

as high as the ivy that grew up from the ground floor to cover the brick facade complete with windows and through which I once saw the hosts fly, the ones the ethereal woman and I consumed; she created a temple with the music of Mozart and Beethoven, with incense, with a few translucent, white doves which, at the hour of meditation, transferred their movement to the music of Kitaro and halted their flight, pausing, with their wings outstretched in that small sitting-room into which was crowded all of Lhasa, Potala, and the white clothing that covered us, those loose, straight shirts and those wide trousers, tied at the waist, that allowed us to form, almost perfectly, the lotus flower; in that profound, silent silence, the wheel, that chakra, the star, which turned on its point of light in the very center of our forehead and from this turning point we departed to ascend to the Master although we knew that we would not yet be allowed to meet him, we only reached Mount Abu from whose heights we contemplated other mountains, to allow the clouds to hit us in the face with their health, with their humid liberation, with their already free reality, although we knew that there was more, much more, on the inaccessible heights where density did not exist and where, for the moment, entry was denied to us; with the last note of *Silk Road*, we returned to our forehead, to the point of light energized by the meditation and then we wandered through that apartment with wooden floors, with its brick facade hugged by the ivy in which I once counted up to ten windows, one long passage, two bedrooms and various other rooms; there, through that subdivided space, we wandered with our white clothes and we told ourselves that the light resided in us; at other times we seated ourselves, face to face, always in lotus position, and we gave ourselves drishti, the transmission of energy through corresponding invisible vessels: the looks we exchanged; until energy beat against our pupils and ran across our faces, liquid, intense, until something touched the chakra of our hearts letting us know that it was the hour of peace, that we could wander calmly, in our white clothes, to each of the corners of this ivy house, to each of the corners of this house of windows, until, in the kitchen, seated at the table made of glass and white iron, we drank jasmine tea that made us wear a mask of humid steam and aroma, and it all lasted until the day everything began to slip away, stealthily, out of the windows: the white clothes, the incense, the sounds of Kitaro and everything else lined up, ready to move out; I think that maybe everything disappeared out of the front windows surrounded by ivy; through there, perhaps that was also where the look you kept in your eyes went, and your forehead of light, and the smooth movement with which you used to smile, because that was where I stood for many months after your disappearance; it was somehow intuitive, it was a painful magnet that was drawing me to the window on the right and that was where I sat so still, awaiting your return with an anguish that became silence; I saw, literally, the mechanism of the passage of time; I watched space crossed by the rain; I watched the feeble snow, falling, freezing everything, perhaps despite itself, drenching everything in its path; and I watched, literally, the non-return; and I saw, literally, the moment when the windows and the doors and the walls enclosed an empty space; and I witnessed, literally, the moment when the other voice was only the sound of my own voice; and I saw, literally, the moment in which the footsteps which trod the wood, were the echo of my own footsteps and nothing more and full stop and silence and absence, until one day it left me, with hardly any movement, almost imperceptibly, with hardly any warning, that painful magnet that drew me to the window, and I stopped waiting; around that time I tried some clumsy steps on the stairway, which was more of a narrow passage descending in terraces, and in the landing, to the left, immediately after the door to the apartment, was the Erasmus that Holbein had painted so many years before and that announced insistently: Piermont Morgan Library, April 21 - July 30; Erasmus's look reaffirmed me: yes, it was the moment to begin to walk, the moment to know that the pain deposited in the lumbar region like a sword slash that had also caught the right leg, was a reminder that something inside us breaks, that we break, while it is expected of us -it's the law of the cosmos, it's the law of the wheel of time - that we continue walking, with or without spare parts, keeping so closely, so close to the windows on the heart, an empty sack; Erasmus was right there, with his skew look placed there by Holbein's hands, whose last brush stroke ended, perhaps one cold day, when the rain fell frozen, when the snow froze everything despite itself, drenching everything in its path; it was then that I committed myself to the descent, leaning on the balustrade, making sure that my foot, as it descended, didn't fall into space by mistake; at the bottom of the stairs, walk a few steps and there is the exit; it was then that the sporadic search began, disorganised, dispassionate and even alien, on the asphalt, in the windows of the train that roared in the belly of the earth; something that I could pick up without anyone seeing that, in that apparently so ingenuous movement of my hand, I hid my hunger, that shame which abandonment brings, that shame brought on by the disappearance of everything that we love, of everything that we once were, a disappearance that leaves us incapable of finding ourselves, because that is how it happened, returning from this haphazard march, I knew and I realized that into that apartment, when the door opened to the circular movement of my hand, no-one went in: my feet walked hidden in their sneakers, but they no longer supported my interior architecture; there was no-one there, nothing, only these bunches of vegetables that I pulled up so secretly and haphazardly, the vaporization at the table from which the steam of jasmine had disappeared and then, to absorb all of this through my nails, but my hunger continued unabated and the emptiness too, the empty sack, so close to my heart; and it was then when I began to devour everything: two Italian coffeepots, one small and the other with an eight cup capacity, the loose shelves of a bookcase supported by three columns of bricks, a china cupboard which was, precisely, in the kitchen and in which we could see, behind the glass, our best loved cups, and the bureau that you gave me, with its roll-back top; all of this in the privacy of my own home, behind closed doors and the unexpected surprise: my hunger persisted; haphazardly, in the art galleries on Madison Avenue, I searched without being seen for a few roots, tubers, leaves, behind the paintings by Francis Bacon, by Botero, the sculptures by More: everything was clean, not a leaf; I returned to the asphalt, to the train windows, to the railings, if only to convince myself that these life forms, so scarce and of little variety, had ceased to exist through disinterest, through a lack of incentive; it was then that I descended to that deepest station and waited for the train, the subway train, the subte-sub, the below-earth train, subterranean, and I opened my mouth so as to make it enormous, immense, infinite, immeasurable, incalculable, and to swallow all the wagons, the first wagon with its light to one side of its forehead and its letters, IRT, destination anywhere, from Manhattan to Sunnyside, from Manhattan to wherever; my mouth opened like a universe and it began closing little by little when faced with the promise of hunger: nothing would fill this space; and I began swallowing that noise, just the noise, like a thin thread of roaring sound that fell into my emptiness, like a bolt of lightening; the train with its wagons and its people hanging from the straps had passed; it was a dizzy and inaccessible passage, it was a noisy, dehumanised speed; I shrugged, climbed the stairs, left through the mouth of the tunnel; the afternoon was cold, very cold, and I, wearing an expression of ingenuousness and innocence so that nobody would notice my abandonment; and I told myself confidently, with certainty, that the search had lasted one year and four months and that everything was the same: the empty sack stuck so closely to my heart, the emptiness of my soul that had decided to move into all the space between my throat and my stomach; I walked along a few streets that were familiar and, at the same time, unknown; the afternoon was cold and this turned into the cold of night; I pushed open the door to the bar and everything stayed behind; the line of stools was still there, parallel to the bar counter; at my side, on the left, one, two, three, four empty stools; on the fifth, a woman almost doubled over the counter, her hand hugging a tall glass that seemed to contain gin; she turned to look at me and I recognised her: she had taken part, just as I had, in some of those pseudo literary meetings in which a group of us -always the same people- read our poetry to the other group that was also always the same; I knew her name and I knew it well, but the only thing that came to mind was the nickname, Skinny, that appeared as if new, in that precise moment, or perhaps it came to me like the remainder of a memory that we can't always place; she straightened her tensed shoulders as much as she was able, moved slightly away from the bar; her movement, a mixture of slow self-confidence and helplessness: I have been waiting for you for eight years, I heard her say, yes, eight years of carrying around this obsession, until I couldn't bear it any more and I went to see you in the hospital and there I convinced myself, when I spoke to you for so many hours about unrelated things, about things that had nothing to do with this moment right now that had to arrive, we spoke about the hole that they had opened in your back, your lumbar disk, that you mentioned so biologically, and I spoke endlessly about my divorce, about my upcoming divorce, and I filled the room with all that had nothing to do with what I wanted to say to you; her voice was strange, extremely strange, almost nasal, and as if, on the way out of her throat, it received hard blows, hammer blows, followed by a thrust of the tongue; her body, bent over like Picasso's ironing woman; she took my hand, we walked to the taxi rank despite my protest that I would be leaving to take up the invitation that arrived for me in a notice in the *New York Times:* "in a far away country we need somebody with your qualifications," qualifications that I had never cared about, but which in this particular case placed me at the head of all those invited; I ended up letting myself be led by the hand, following her strange voice: these months with me will help you not to feel alone when you leave, they will help me not to feel alone when I stay behind; we took a taxi which took us to Astoria; the apartment was on the ground floor, light and welcoming, sprinkled with the voice of the magic child, with her absolute charm, with her incredible wisdom and whom I would hear, so many times, weeks later, ask from the bath: Mommy, Mommy, and this silence? are you getting married?; this definitive visit started us on the habit of touring the city, of walking through it sometimes with the child between the two of us, each of her hands held tightly by ours, and we would walk around the Village; at other times we went on adventures without the little girl, these included a visit to the

Jacques Marchais Center for Tibetan Art on Staten Island where we watched a performance by the Yueh Lung Shadow Theatre with several plays: *The Two Friends, The Crane and the Tortoise, The Mountain of Firey Tongues;* the South Street Seaport with its cobbled streets and strong smell of the Fulton Fish Market; to cross the Brooklyn Bridge, to go to the Kabuki, to some Manhattan museum or to arm ourselves with blankets, books and snacks and to spend hours in Central Park, always looking for the corner where the Black singer would stand, a busker that sang nostalgic songs in French, accompanying himself with his guitar; the sunny days at the end of March bringing with them happiness in their maelstrom of walks, dinners in different restaurants, a movie and, upon our return, that magic child with her stories and her fabulous imagination, and I too with my stories and the tales that I read aloud to her and the programmes on television that we discussed with such seriousness and all the charm and the joy of that small enchantress until she was finally overcome with sleep and it was time to put her to bed in her tiny bed surrounded by toys, and the night then jumped to a cup of camomile, to a Lady Godiva chocolate, to the smoke of incense, to the music of Kitaro that, once again, provided the background; the room in the corner, the light from the street lamps, the noise of an occasional car, all filtering into the room, filtering into the woman's leanness, adding itself to her tenderness, to her wild love, watching her riding the night that made her almost beautiful, almost so beautiful, nearly beautiful; her homely body became poetry, as did the breadth of my body, -sculptural as you said,- until sunrise surprised us; one unexpected day, perhaps, forgetfulness began to call on you, the forgetfulness that our eternal pact would last exactly, approximately, nearly, a few months; a forgetfulness that began to watch my every step, my walk, my voice, the direction of my pupils; this forgetfulness stretched to your hands, into your hands, from your hands to grab hold of me; in order to grow in the very corners where your generosity, like that of a lean panther that prowls at night, grew, and I never spoke, I was unable to do so, of my tenderness, when you reclaimed me with the violence of a Parisian Tango, in your passionate and gratuitous jealous scenes, because I knew, knew perfectly and knew well, that from your pile of bones, today, there shouted your childhood of nine years, the exact point at which the militiamen made your mother disappear in order to hide her in a prison for five years, the exact point at which they made your father disappear to hide him in another prison, for ten years; and you were left on your own, wandering from house to house, wandering from unlove to unlove, wandering from abandonment to abandonment, in Santiago, old capital of the Oriente Province, where you paid the price for being the daughter of parents baptised with the name of counter-revolutionaries; and I watched as your panther skin literally stretched, glowing in the dark; I saw, literally, that your pain stretched like the long skin of a leopard; I saw, literally, when you would coil around me, for me, towards me, in tears, in pain, in tenderness, in forgetfulness of a pact on fragmented time, to keep me company, remember? to keep you company; so that I wouldn't feel alone when I left, remember? so that you wouldn't feel alone when you stayed behind; it all happened one morning, very early; you were in the sitting-room, framed in the centre of a doorway and a moan began to emanate from you which turned into water, currents of water, violent water, whirling water that filled everything, that pulled at everything, that flowed through the angle formed by your legs, through the open space of your arms, through your immobile body, always framed in the doorway; until the flow of water became hurt, docile, still, and you became sun; everything dried out, in a cleansed quietness; we left for the airport and you watched me disappear at the sound of the voice: flight SAA 202 to Johannesburg; it was July then, the twelfth thereof the town was in an uproar because word had gone out: what Peter had been looking for so many years in so many litanies, was the formula for definitive death and, what was even more astounding and, one could even say, a little shocking, was his complete hermeticism about something he should have considered to be of general concern, for everyone, in everyone, from everyone, because after all, death is not an elitist thing because we all pass that way and have always done so, but what was most mortifying was that some had come to consider him as the True One and had even begun to believe that he was a prophet and visionary that had come to this world to teach them a spatial-temporal multiplicity, as the owner of Ricardo's Press, who is always to be trusted, had explained; people had also begun to say that he had come to this world to demonstrate to us, to show us and to make us see that death does not exist and that all that we do is to pass from one vibration frequency to another, but what no-one understood, nor had he explained, is why his eyes bulged, why, when he was asked if there was life after death, he carried a twitching and tense hand to his chest and began to knead with his fingers as if he wanted to sink them into what we had one day heard him say was called the chakra of the solar plexus and which we affectionately term here, in this town, the chakra of the heart, which is more or less where we all believe feelings and the soul are located, although he had said, and we believed him because he said it one day when he was alone in the river, that what there is in the heart is a seed which is like a microscopic record of the story of all the lives that we have had and all the lives that we have at present, at the same time and simultaneously; and after kneading with his fingers for a bit, he began to scratch at his chest as if to dig up his heart with its seed and everything, but we never understood what he intended by this and we left it alone, just one more of the many peculiarities that he had; what is surprising and what is upsetting and what cannot be forgiven is that he has made us feel so, so very satisfied with there not being any death and now he comes out with this business of searching for it like that, so definitively; and although they try to defend him by saying that he never tried to convince us to believe this or that, more than once we followed him to the river and there, beneath the bridge, we heard him speaking to himself and we began to feel so, so happy with this thing about there not being any death that we even thought about presenting him officially, and very officially, with the title of the True Giver of Hope, and this was going to be made known publicly on Sunday, in the park, when the band plays, and after handing over a small certificate that we were going to give him, the musicians would immediately and straight away play the national anthem for him; after hearing him shouting so many times that death is not death, we believed it too and we got so used to the idea that just the other day when an uncle of the second cousin to Chicho Bota died, the second cousin said to him as he was about to go to the next world: "being as I am your nephew, I would appreciate it if you could start looking out for a small apartment for me over there, on the other side, so that I don't have to search when it is my turn, and if it's possible, one in the same neighbourhood where you are, because as you already know, uncle, family is family here and anywhere else and all the rest is nonsense," and the day after the funeral the second cousin played a few *guarachas* on the record player and turned it up loud so that his uncle could also enjoy them as he had done for so long, at three in the afternoon between sip after sip of coffee; and the joke of the town was watching the Poles, who owned the store that sells offcuts, and didn't know what to invent so that people would buy that black material that had piled up because, with the story about there not being any death, no one wanted to wear mourning clothes any more; and although he never said so, that is what we thought he was saying to us: "rejoice in the death that is not death;" and when we started to rejoice, this blow arrives, a blow and punch to know that what Peter Matei is searching for is the death that is indeed death; and now this business of vibrating in another frequency can't be so great if he wants to disappear and that is something that cannot be denied to anyone because we found a little booklet that came out of the hollow trunk of the tree near the river, and in Peter's handwriting, that we all recognised, was written: "Alchemy of the word: litanies to find definitive death;" and if this wasn't enough, there was, between the pages of the booklet, a folded, very well folded, parchment in which he stated clearly, very clearly, that he had to reach the end of his centuries of hunger, that it is always the same, the rust which eats at his bones, the sadness that crosses the centre of the medulla with its long tongue; his body that is a skeleton that comes and goes and walks and everything and for what, if his word is not planted, that's what he said, planted in the hearts of others, nor does love embrace him like a blanket bought in Mitla: "because the starving doves arrive to carry off the stones of my blood, and when satiated, they launch a magic flight to search for the light of the stars which I do not possess, and my nails retain a hollow of ocean and a murmur of mountain, an echo on its own that comes to carve corners on my shoulder so that the kiss of morning cannot land there; an enormous eye, in the doorway of my navel always watched with surprise: the conviction that one will know love, of being able to point to it with one's finger, to know that it had been, that it was, that it was being, but perhaps not completely, but perhaps never enough, because I watched it refined to the point of transparency, so often till transparency and then I watched them fly, the doves flew, escaping towards the light with my stones in their beaks, unlearning to love me;" well, and it continues with other things, but what we must understand is that it is not enough that a few of us have followed him because he doesn't even mention us or acknowledge our recognition of him, and as if this weren't enough, to complain that no-one loves him when we who are the voice of the town, and the town itself, have always been considerate towards him, and a good day, Peter, how are you, Peter, was never lacking; but if he has never learned to accept this, right here we declare: "we, who are the town's voice, suggest to you that you go and look for some other vibration; it was our intention and our wish to tolerate your presence that we secretly rejected; with our shared effort and our good intentions, you never lack for a good day, Peter, nor a how are you, Peter; and even one small group amongst us became interested in hearing what you had to say, but this business of waiting for someone to embrace you like a blanket, no way, not from Mitla nor from any other place and, in short, we say that if you want to leave here, we will not stop you;" Quico and Mayito, the two apprentices in the Printing Shop spent hours during the night multiplying flyers headed with large black letters like newspaper headlines: TO PETER MATEI, and below that, DECLARATION BY THE TOWN'S VOICE, and thereafter the declaration in red letters; Quico and Mayito left just before dawn and covered the town sticking up flyers in passageways, windows, poles, shops, buildings, sidewalks, trees, river banks, the river itself, because what was important was not to inform the sons of the Guaso, who already knew about it, but to ensure that at some moment Peter would come across one of the flyers and that he would read it and that he would know then and to the depths of his being, what was expected of him; with daybreak, the two strapping youths began to feel the tiredness brought on by a night without sleep and the distance covered which had began to seem interminable to them; they were almost at the crossroads between Pedro A. Pérez Street and Crombet Street when their steps were halted by a tumult of people that swarmed like bees on the sidewalks of the park, the shoe store, the Petit Miami, the furniture store; in the middle of the street, Cuadrado, fuming with rage, had got out of his car in the foul mood that characterised him, he had removed his chauffeur's cap and he waved it furiously in the air: "I sounded the horn but I didn't bother to brake because the klaxon is enough and before I knew it he was already under the wheels;" one of the mayor's assistants came to calm the chauffeur of the only taxi in Guaso Town: "Look, Cuadrado, don't get mad on me, although you are in the right, just because you blasted the horn is no reason to stand there gaping; look, I've brought these jute sacks to wrap the Long in them as best we can, the last thing we need is for him to decide to bleed and to stain the car; wrap him well and take him to the Municipal Hospital which is just at the edge of the town, beyond the cemetery, a mere formality, because this one won't live to tell the tale; let me help you; as you know, we had to send the ambulance to a sugar mill, a cane cutter cut his arm with his machete, a man who is an office worker and he went out to cut cane, wouldn't you know, who would think of doing such a thing, something about being made redundant or I don't know what, anyway, Cuadrado, we will pay you for the trip to the hospital, a mere formality, nothing more;" and I'll tell you, Chachi, something that I've never told you before: despite the pain of knowing that your having fallen in love marked our definitive separation, your falling in love ended up being a solution; something grey and opaque lashed at us for several years; I remember well, very well, that in 1979 I felt as if death had lodged in the hollow of my throat, in the hollow of my heart; a slow and heavy death, Chachi, a death whose weight one felt like a bitter shadow and I ran out into the street, to that wide, South Highland Avenue as if looking for the true death, the one that leads to a definitive disappearance; the years in Sunnyside were marked by horrible pains carved into my spine like a sword wound and by the growth of your boredom that enlarged until that day, very early in November, in that year of 1983 when you answered the ringing phone while I washed the dishes in the kitchen; I heard your sweet voice break, and then I knew; and everything arrived like an avalanche, to tear out those ten years, to know that up to there the story was our story, that perhaps it had always been ours despite everything; with the taste of something definitive came the certainty that it was better that way; the moment in which you would disappear had arrived and with it, the relief of knowing that you would not be alone; I had felt for some time, Chachi, the exact awareness of my inability for desertion, my inability to leave you on your own if you still needed me; the only thing that remained for us to do, Chachi, was to save a memory, to retain the melancholy of absence, but you insisted on staying on, stuck to that apartment, invading it with your new company, and you created your love nest in that sitting-room that years before had been transformed, by your decree, into a sacred temple for meditation; and what hurt most, Chachi, was watching your image crack, undo itself, was watching you diminish as you learnt to destroy, step by step, corner by corner, wall by wall, that space that you would once have defended so fiercely as ours, the bookcases with their planks and bricks fell down, the pointed, wicker, corner cupboard where once golden fish had lived, the portrait of Erasmus, my paintings, your records, it all fell down and became something else, a dense, grey dust from which our footsteps had disappeared; in my room the paper debris increased, the disorder increased and a rain of restless mice, in front of my bed, formed quick wheels that moved in the air like the Bengal lights and it was there, in that moment, when I wanted to feel a wave of clean space that would make me want to shout your name while knowing that you were not coming back; you stayed there until the end of May 1985 when we left, on the same day, that apartment in Sunnyside

SHAMBALLA

Peter grew lighter until he floated off; he arrived at Shamballa just as he had so many times before; he sat down in a chair in the transparency of the atmosphere, his elbows resting on his thighs, his head inclined, between his hands; still seated on his chair, he sat a little straighter when the air became more luminous and transparent; he recognized the Guides that appeared, seated in a circle around him; he recognised the voices raised in unison to create one voice reciting a litany that reached him like a shiver of breath; he recognised the series of affirmations that they repeated with an occasional variation, like an echo:

you were a drawing
a drawing you were

you were a preacher
misguided preacher you were

you were a vizier
dissatisfied and misled vizier you were

you were a slave
dissatisfied slave you were

you were a particle of light in the wheel of the cycles
a particle of light you were in the wheel of the cycles

you were one of humanity's monsters
an arsonist and a monster you were

you were legend
dissatisfied legend you were, you dared to live outside the voice of the amauta and you transformed yourself into mist in the Ollantaitambo

you were emperor
a paranoid emperor you were, a preacher of Confucius and an executioner of those you believed wished you harm

"you were all of these and all are in you now, Peter Matei, and in the other being that hides inside you, that you feel inside of you, although you know that at times that being lives outside of you, almost always in other stations on earth and sometimes in another decade, different to yours, but you feel her just the same because you are the sum of your past and your multiple present shared out over this century, in different times, in different spaces; return, Peter, from this change of frequency that happens to you; return, Peter, so that you learn to forget about definitive death in the same way in which we take from you the memory of this encounter, awake!"

FINAL LITANY

the roots of our blood are of no importance, up to where do they extend, from where do they come, when did their echo begin to form, yesterday, so long ago, now, as I write, in the right hand corner of this off-white paper, a date, July, the nineteenth, the year I must call 1979, a footnote in this wheel in which I never lose my awareness of being; so many days, weeks, time pushing itself, squeezing itself into lumps, heaps of flat minutes and seconds, smooth; now everything recedes, everything is going away and leaving me in a strange time, leaving me in a borrowed space; this woman that shares my breath, my way of breathing, also leaves, so often I look at her and she has already gone, and her voice and her silhouette are echoes that have been left behind; everything recedes, the apartment goes, and I walk and wander around these premises with the same number, 87 South Highland, on the same second floor, the letter B still there, the number 25 stuck on the door as if it were a trade mark that has lost its impact, its validity, a means of identification; and I am not here either, although in the village they still recognize me as Peter the Long, as Peter the Wanderer, and they don't know, they know nothing of the interminable search through so many centuries for a method to perfect death so as to make it definitive, I'm following data and formulas that beat at my Alchemist's brain, because the secret is in the bath, in those ancient tiles, in the porcelain bathtub, in the whiteness that allows itself to be discerned beneath the water, and that is what they give to me, the formula, Peter, the lukewarm water, and you, naked, bend down, curl up like a fetus, hug your knees, tightly, so that your shoulder blades stick out, and like this, in silence, await the definitive death; but the hours pass and the water loses its warmth and the alchemist voices abandon the tiles, they cease beating at my brain, and something insipid rises in my throat while the towelling sucks the humidity from this skin that I do not understand, because I am not here, but I have not died because I do not feel myself travelling across space; I must continue, early tomorrow morning, walking the streets of the village, searching for alchemist sounds, the formula for definitive death; because when numbness sets in, at the hour of the near find, I am left with this awareness of nothingness, of this function that is not noted, that passes without footprints on the banks of sand; the village voices interrupt the message, there goes Peter the Wanderer, Peter the Long, with his distant gaze; and they do not know the secret of the search, and they do not know that these eyes that lose themselves are antennas that record, that take note of what remains of me, all this that does not count: a hollow, a bitter leftover in the chest of this being that has not finished tearing up its accumulation of selves that persist in retaining material existence, a point of reference for the pain, for this lack of desire for life that continues to grow in me without realising that I once had a strong will, I possessed it, I was able to manage simple things: the mechanics of getting up when the alarm went off, to earn a salary, to pay rent, to write a book in reply, a cryptic answer, an hieroglyphic if you will, but, in any case, something that I would have to describe as a voice; and now the discouragement and the ended search, and the closed doors, and the knock of fists that begin to weaken until persistence becomes an ethereal thing, a knock without validity, an empty mechanism, empty of hope, of energy, of the purifying symptom of breathing and I tell myself, Peter, the Wanderer, look, Peter the Long, exhaustion falls on you today but alchemy is in the air, in the voices of the fine rain; and now, the steps before me, and the doors of the church, and the empty corridors, and these ancient stones that guard the dust between the cracks, and the ivy that I see embracing its walls, and these empty pews, and before the altar, the long box, the planks covered with the remains of grey paint, and the unlit candles there, waiting, at the foot of the planks; I know it is time and I lay down the length of my body made to fit the wood, and the voices dictate to me and now I have the formula I must repeat until I disappear: "I am a shell knocking on the doors, and it's fine like that, it would be fine if this half eaten hollow didn't exist, if this pain were not so dryly mine, if this resignation were not so identifiable, if I were not ..."